Daniel

The sequel to *Shelter*

ROBIN MERRILL

New Creation Publishing

New Creation Publishing
Madison, Maine

This novel is a work of fiction. Names, characters, businesses, organizations, places, events, and incidents are either the products of the author's imagination or used in a fictitious manner. Any resemblance to actual persons, living or dead, or actual events is purely coincidental.

Scripture quotations taken from the New American Standard Bible®, Copyright © 1960, 1962, 1963, 1968, 1971, 1972, 1973, 1975, 1977, 1995 by The Lockman Foundation. Used by permission. (www.Lockman.org)

Cover photo by Lisa Berry
Cover design by Rachel McColl, Taste & See Design
Formatting by Perry Elisabeth Design | perryelisabethdesign.com

Library of Congress Control Number: 2016909912
ISBN-13: 978-0692741139
ISBN-10: 0692741135

For my first and favorite reader. Thanks, Mom.

Chapter 1

Pastor Dan died on his namesake's eighth birthday. When young Daniel heard the news, his blue eyes filled with tears as he said, "But I'm not ready yet."

At fifty-two, Pastor Dan was young for heart failure. Maggie, the unofficial church secretary, found him on a Tuesday morning. He usually walked across the small church parking lot from his parsonage to the church around nine. When lunchtime came and Maggie hadn't seen him, she ventured out to the parsonage herself. It wasn't that she was worried about him, but the crises were piling up, and she needed his help.

But she found him lying on his couch as if he'd fallen asleep watching television. Before she realized he was gone, she marveled at the carefree look on his face. For a man who spent his days sprinting from one calamity to the next, Pastor Dan always seemed fundamentally at peace.

Maggie called the paramedics. Then she called her husband Galen. He beat the ambulance there and wrapped his thick arms around his wife.

"What are we going to do?" she mumbled into his chest.

He seemed to think about that for a few seconds before sighing. "I have no idea."

She looked up at him. "We have to tell the people. They'll flood out of the church when they see the ambulance."

Galen sighed again. "You're right. You want me to do it?"

"No, it's OK. I'll go. Can you stay here and wait for the EMTs?"

Galen kissed his wife on the top of the head, nodded, and then let her go.

Tiny met Maggie at the door. Tiny, as is so often the case with a nickname like that, was a giant of a man. Maggie had once confided in Galen that Tiny reminded her of Lennie from *Of Mice and Men*, which would make her George. Tiny had made himself Maggie's unofficial assistant and bodyguard. At first, this had annoyed Maggie, but she had grown used to him now and appreciated him more every day.

"You're crying," Tiny said when he saw her.

"Yes, I know," Maggie said and wiped at her eyes with the backs of her hands. "Can you please go round everyone up? We need to have a family meeting."

"Sure, Maggie," Tiny said. And he was off.

Maggie heard the sirens then and knew that those would draw people as fast as Tiny's roundup. She made her way to the front of the sanctuary and watched people file in.

Open Door Church was a small church in the small town of Mattawooptock, Maine. The church also served as a homeless shelter, but it wasn't particularly crowded this September. It was rarely crowded there during the warm months. Many people who had no place else to go preferred sleeping outside, in tents, or in cars to sleeping at a church. Pastor Dan's only rule was that guests of the church had to go to Bible study every night, and even though that wasn't much of a requirement, it still kept plenty of people away, when they had other options.

Still, about forty people were staying at Open Door at the time of Dan's death, including several families. Maggie nodded at her friend Harmony when she entered the sanctuary. Harmony gave her a stoic nod in return. Harmony had been living at the church long enough to know that these impromptu meetings were rarely for good news.

"Thanks for coming, everyone. I'll make this quick, and I don't have any answers at this point, so please don't bombard me with questions. As soon as I learn anything, I will pass it on to you all." She took a deep breath and tried to steady her voice, "Pastor Dan has gone home to be with the Lord."

All around the room, jaws dropped. A few of the women—and Tiny—burst into tears. Then the hands started going up.

"Who's going to be our pastor?" Zane asked.

"What happened to him?" John called from the back row.

"What's going to happen to us?" Melanie cried out from the front.

Maggie put her hands up. "Like I said, guys, I don't know anything at this point. Please, just be patient, and I will do my absolute best to keep you informed."

People kept firing questions at her, but she left the sanctuary and headed for the office. When she got there, she shut the door behind her. Immediately, Tiny opened it again and followed her in. But then he shut it behind him and silently took a seat. Maggie sat down behind the desk and put her head in her hands.

After a few minutes, she turned her attention back to the computer screen, where she had been rearranging the laundry schedule. She stared at that until there was a soft knock on the door. She looked up.

Her good friend Pete stuck his head in. "Sorry, Maggie, but we've got new guests. Can I send them in?"

Maggie nodded and stood to greet them.

Pete disappeared for a second and then returned with two women and three children. "Hi, I'm Maggie," Maggie said, and held out her hand to one of the women. "Welcome to Open Door Church. We're glad you're here. Would you like to have a seat?"

The woman nodded. There weren't enough chairs for everyone; Maggie nodded to Tiny, who reluctantly got up and offered his seat to the other woman, who was holding a tiny baby in her arms.

Maggie pulled out the necessary paperwork. "What are your names?"

"I'm Brenda," the older woman said. "This is my daughter Bailey, my son Brad, and my daughter Breanna, and that," she said, pointing to the baby in Breanna's arms, "is my granddaughter Ava."

"Welcome," Maggie said again. "Let's see if we can't get you all into the same room."

Once Maggie had the newcomers settled, she returned to the office to find her husband waiting for her.

"You OK?" Galen asked.

"Not sure yet. What on earth are we going to do?"

Galen looked at the floor. "No idea."

"I mean, it honestly never occurred to me that Dan could die. What is God thinking? How can this place survive without him?"

Galen sighed. "I don't know. I guess it will survive if God wants it to survive. And as for what God's thinking, maybe he's thinking Dan needed a break. Maybe this is the only way God could get him to take one."

Maggie smiled at that. "Yeah, he sure did deserve one, didn't he?"

They sat quietly for a few minutes, each apparently lost in thought. Then Maggie broke the silence. "So I guess we should plan a funeral, right? We should write an obituary? Does Dan have any family who should be doing these things? Or at least someone we should call?"

Galen shook his head. "I know his wife was local, so maybe we should call her family. I know he kept in touch with them after she died. As for Dan, I never heard him talk about his own folks or siblings. I never heard him talk about himself much at all."

"Isn't that the truth? OK, I'll find out how to get in touch with his wife's family. Maybe they can tell us more. But Galen, we're going to need a pastor. How exactly do we begin that search? It's not like we're a mainline denomination with a diocese in control."

Galen smiled ruefully. "Listen to you with all your church talk."

Maggie rolled her eyes. "Look, I've been at this a while now. But really, what does a non-denominational, independent church do? Do we just put an ad in the paper? And what do we have to offer a prospective pastor? Did Dan have benefits? How much did he get paid? *How* did he get paid for that matter?"

"I don't think he did."

"You can't be serious."

"I mean, I don't think Dan had drawn a paycheck in years. He just lived like his guests. He ate the food that was given to the church. He wore the clothes that were given to the church. He never took a vacation. He never bought new shoes. I don't think he got paid."

Maggie let out a low whistle. "Wow, I guess I never thought about it. So how on earth are we going to replace him? How are we going to find someone who will work for free?"

"I don't know," Galen said. "Maybe we can't. Maybe we have to figure out a way to pay someone. Maybe we start with appointing someone treasurer."

"You mean someone *other* than Pastor Dan?"

"Yeah, that's what I mean. Good grief, he really did it all, didn't he?" Galen paused. He ran his fingers through his short, dark hair and studied the floor some more. After a minute of that, he looked up abruptly. "You know, I think we must have some bylaws around here somewhere from when the church first formed. I mean, we're a nonprofit, right? So there must be an official board somewhere?"

Maggie snorted. "A board of homeless people?"

"Well no, this church didn't start out as a homeless shelter. It started out as just a church. Maybe those bylaws would have some procedure in place. Better than nothing?" Galen said hopefully.

"You know what?" Maggie said, with a hint of hope in her voice for the first time that morning.

Galen shook his head.

"We should call Cari."

Galen slapped the table. "Yes! Yes, we should. Call Cari. Right now."

"Somerset County Career Center. How may I direct your call?" a tired voice answered.

"Is Cari available?" Maggie asked.

"Hold please."

Cari had been Maggie before Maggie was Maggie. Or rather, Cari had done the job Maggie had been trying to do ever since Cari left for greener pastures. Cari had served at Open Door tirelessly until she got a job doing employment counseling. Her new job was a huge boost to the shelter, as she took special care to help church guests find jobs and get back on their feet—or in some cases, on their feet for the first time.

"This is Cari."

"Hey, Cari, it's Maggie."

"Oh hey, Maggs! Long time no chat. What's up?"

"Are you sitting down?" Maggie asked.

"No time. Just spill it."

"Pastor Dan. He's gone."

"What do you mean he's gone?"

"I mean he's gone." Maggie's voice cracked. "He died this morning. Or sometime last night. I found him this morning."

Cari was silent.

"You OK?"

"Nope."

"I'm sorry to tell you like this, but Galen and I need your help. Do you know if Dan had any family? Someone we should call?"

"Just his wife's folks."

"Do you know their names?"

Cari rattled them off, along with their address. Maggie scribbled them down.

"And do you know if we have any church bylaws or anything? Is there any procedure in place for how to hire a new pastor? And I'm not even sure we should use the word 'hire.' I mean, did Dan even get paid?"

Cari sighed. "No, he didn't get paid. If he needed something, he would ask me if there was enough money for it in the safe. If there wasn't, he went without. If there was, then he helped himself. But we're talking a tank of gas or a new toothbrush. It's not like he was buying snowmobiles."

"I know," Maggie said.

"It was all very laid back," Cari explained. "Dan feels, or *felt* I guess, that God was in control of the money. So he didn't pay much attention to it. It was always there when we really needed it. But I'm not sure how that system's going to work now. Most people expect a little more organization when money is involved."

"I think—" Maggie started, but Cari immediately interrupted.

"As for bylaws, yeah, they're there, but they're wicked old, and probably completely useless at this point. Look on Dan's bookshelf. They are in a black binder. I suppose you, or we, or someone, should form a hiring committee and hope God will send us someone. I don't see what else you can do. Unless G wants to take over."

Maggie chuckled humorlessly. She looked at her husband sitting quietly on the other side of the desk. "Do you know how many times I've heard Galen say, 'I don't know how Dan does it'?" Galen frowned.

"True. But Dan's not going to be doing it anymore," Cari said.

"OK, I'll go find the binder and see what we can figure out. Thanks, Cari."

"You bet. Keep me in the loop. I'll be praying."

"Thanks," Maggie said. "Bye." She hung up.

"Cari wants me to do it?" Galen said, looking aghast.

"No, she just mentioned it as an option."

"Well, why don't we get the funeral set up first? Then we'll worry about finding a new pastor. Until then, I can fill in where needed." Galen stood up to leave. "God help us all."

"Does that mean you're doing Bible study tonight?" Maggie called after him.

"Well, tonight is my turn anyway," Galen said without turning around.

Chapter 2

Hundreds of people showed up for the funeral. The sanctuary was packed. Every seat was full and people were lined up along each wall, standing quietly in the stuffy late-summer heat. Maggie and Galen sat near the front with their two sons, Isaiah (seven) and Elijah (five), perched on their laps. Latecomers stood in the foyer, mostly unable to see or hear anything.

Galen had asked a pastor from Waterville, someone he'd heard Dan speak highly of, to officiate the service, and he did a bang-up job. He read some Scriptures on heaven, shared a brief but poignant Gospel message, and then opened the floor to anyone who wanted to share. And boy, did they. Soul after soul took the microphone and shared how Dan had saved their lives, how he'd helped them get clean, how he'd led them to the Lord, how he'd believed in them when no one else did. Then little Daniel asked for the microphone.

Daniel had practically grown up at Open Door. Pastor Dan had been at the hospital when Harmony had delivered Daniel, and Pastor had driven them home to the church when they were discharged. Since then, Harmony and Daniel had moved out of the shelter a few times, in various attempts to live on their own, but something had always gone wrong, and they kept returning to Open Door, where they currently lived.

"Except for my Father in heaven," young Daniel began, sounding remarkably composed for an eight-year-old, "Pastor Dan was the only father I've ever known. I am glad I do not know my real father, because I had Pastor Dan. He taught me so much about the Bible and about fishing. I will try to make him proud with my life."

Maggie had managed to keep it together until then, but at Daniel's words, the dam broke, and she began to sob into the top of Elijah's head. If Pastor Dan had been Daniel's father, then she was his aunt. She and Daniel's mother Harmony had been close friends for a long time. Harmony had been Maggie's first roommate when Maggie had first arrived at the shelter, lost, alone, and scared.

After the funeral, most of the people trickled downstairs to the kitchen for refreshments. The room wasn't big enough for so many visitors, but at least it was cooler down there. It soon became evident that the normal kitchen staff was overwhelmed at the task, and, briefly, Maggie wondered if Pastor Dan would jump in and get things under control. Of course, she soon realized that he wouldn't, so she told Galen he was in charge of their children, and put on an apron herself.

When her husband and tired children were ready to leave, she was just getting started on the dishes. "Go ahead," she said to Galen. "I'll be home as soon as I can."

Galen gave her a kiss on the cheek and then whispered in her ear. "Hurry, though, OK? I'd like to go over my notes one more time for the sermon tomorrow." Then he vanished, leaving her with her rubber gloves in the air so the water didn't run into them.

"What's wrong?" Pete asked.

"Oh, nothing's wrong. I'm just feeling torn. I need to help here, but Galen needs me to help at home."

"Go home. We'll be fine," Pete said. Just then, Maggie and Pete both heard Jessica cuss out a funeral guest they didn't recognize. Maggie rushed over to defuse the situation, and Pete returned to cutting up more watermelon.

Maggie and the cranky kitchen crew scurried around serving the guests for two hours. At one point, Tiny asked Maggie, "Are these people ever going to leave?"

"Not sure?" Maggie said.

"Well, can we kick them out?" Tiny asked. "I'm tired."

"Not sure," Maggie said again. "I think that would be bad form."

Eventually, people did leave, and Maggie, Jessica, and Pete finished up cleaning the kitchen, while Tiny stood watch at the door.

"Don't work too hard, Tiny," Pete said.

"Hush," Maggie muttered to Pete. "If he helps too much, he'll just get in the way, and you know that."

With the kitchen clean and the light off, Maggie dragged herself up the stairs and then out to her car. Maggie and her family lived in an apartment over her husband's garage. It was cozy, but the price was right.

When she got home, she found the apartment strangely quiet and her husband staring at his Bible.

"Everything OK?" she asked.

"Yeah," Galen whispered. "The boys fell asleep, thank God. Apparently grief exhausts them. I'm just going over my notes. I'm nervous about tomorrow. I don't want anyone to think I'm trying to take over or anything."

"It's OK, honey," Maggie said. She kissed him on the temple and then began to rub his shoulders. "You'll be terrific. It's not like you didn't try to find someone else to do it, right? Just try to give it to God and let the Holy Spirit do his thing."

Galen looked up at her with an amused look on his face.

"What?" she said, stopping her massage.

"Oh nothing. It's just funny to hear my own advice coming back at me from my wife's lips."

Maggie quietly giggled. "Well, it's good advice," she said and wrapped her arms around him. "Come on, let's go to bed. Morning will come soon."

Maggie and Galen got to church early the next morning and were greeted by four men neither of them recognized. The men were all wearing suits.

"Good morning," one of them said, and held out a hand to Galen, who took it. "Welcome to Open Door Church."

"And you are?" Galen asked.

"I am Phil Miller. I'm an elder here at Open Door."

Maggie sucked in some air while her husband belted out a laugh. "Oh? You are? I didn't realize we had any elders?"

The man's smile didn't fade. "Well, church politics you know, but that's all behind us now. I'd like to introduce you to Open Door's new pastor, Christian Hatch."

The man beside Phil the elder stepped forward. "Chris, please," he said taking Galen's hand. "Pleasure to meet you."

"Maggie, would you take the kids into the sanctuary, please?" Galen asked in a strained tone. Hurriedly, Maggie complied. When his family had vanished, Galen said, "I'm sorry, but I've been regularly attending and serving in this church for more than a decade and I've never seen any of you. How could you possibly have chosen a new pastor without any input from the church members? And how could you have done this in a week?"

"Yes," Phil said, "we moved swiftly as soon as we heard the sad news about Dan. We can't have a church without a shepherd, now can we?"

Galen's face grew red. "I don't think you understand what I'm asking. Who *are* you people? You can't just come in off the street and hire a pastor!"

Phil gave Galen what appeared to be a practiced, plastic smile. "We are not off the street. We are the elders of this church, chosen by the church membership, apparently before you started attending here. We understand change is hard, but—"

"Change is hard?" Galen was almost shouting now, and the new pastor took a step back. "Are you out of your mind?"

Maggie reappeared then. She looked fairly composed until she saw the look on her perpetually calm husband's face. Then she looked distressed. She was carrying a pen and notebook. "Could I have your names please?" she asked the men in suits.

"Certainly," Phil replied. "I am Phil Miller. This here is Elder Albert Pelotte, and this is Elder George Clifford."

Maggie scribbled the names down. "You didn't need to repeat the word elder. We are well aware of the point you are trying to make."

"You calling Cari?" Galen asked Maggie.

"Yes, and I'm checking the bylaws to see if they speak to any part of this scenario."

"Oh, they do," Phil interjected. "I wrote the bylaws."

Speechless, Maggie unlocked the office and Galen followed her in, shutting the door behind him.

"Where did you put the kids?" he asked.

"They're in the sanctuary. I told them they could play with my phone if they were silent."

"Well, you're going to need a new phone."

Maggie dialed Cari's home number.

"Hello?" a groggy voice answered.

"Hey, it's Maggie. We have a problem."

Cari snorted. "We always have a problem. Couldn't it wait until my alarm went off?"

"No, this is way bigger than most of our problems. Do you know Phil Miller, Albert Pelotte, George Clifford, or Christian Hatch?"

Cari groaned. "I know the first three names, but not the last. Why? They're not there are they?"

"Yes, they are, and they're claiming to be elders and they've hired a new pastor, this Christian Hatch guy, who looks like he's about twenty-five. And they're all wearing *ties*!" Maggie said as if that was the most exasperating part of the whole affair.

"I'll be right there."

True to her word, Cari got to church within about fifteen minutes, looking disheveled and ornery. "Well, this is a blast from the past," Maggie whispered to Galen.

They met her at the door, just as the new welcoming committee attempted to greet her.

"Don't bother, Phil," Cari said as Phil extended his hand in greeting. "You may not remember me, but I remember you all too well."

"I'm sorry," Phil said, still smiling. "Have I had the pleasure?"

"What, are you running for office or something? Cut the act, Phil." Then Cari looked at Galen. "These folks *were* our church elders. But when Dan opened the doors to the homeless, they made a big stink about it. And when they couldn't get their way, they formed a new church in Winslow. What's going on *there* this morning? Who is running that dog and pony show if you're here?" Cari spat.

"Now, now," Phil said to Cari without taking his eyes off Galen. "That's not an entirely accurate depiction of events. We weren't against lending a helping hand. We just disagreed with Dan about how to go about it."

"Whatever," Cari snapped. "It's all ancient history now. What are you doing *here*? What could you possibly want with us now? You know there are still homeless people here?"

"If I may," the young new pastor stepped forward. "I do want this job. I am ready for it, and I have a heart for the homeless. If you'll just give me a chance."

"Have you heard what it pays?" Galen asked.

"Yes, we've taken care of that," Phil answered. "We've offered him a competitive package."

"A package made of what?" Galen asked, clearly astonished. "Last Tuesday everyone ate green beans for supper because that's all there was! Are you going to pay him in canned vegetables?"

Phil sighed. "Dan wasn't skilled at raising or managing funds. That is no secret. But we are. I have an MBA, Albert here is an accountant, and George here has successfully run his own business for years. We have the skills to take this place to the next level."

Galen rubbed his temples. "This can't be happening."

"Look, we know change is hard. We know you are grieving. But we are your elders and we ask you to respect that. Why don't you go find a seat in the sanctuary and spend some time asking God to calm your spirits before the service begins?"

Galen stood still for several long seconds, just staring at the man in front of him. Then he took a deep breath and went into the sanctuary. Cari followed. Maggie went to lock up the office. When she rejoined Galen and Cari, Isaiah and Elijah were crawling all over Galen as if they hadn't seen him in days. He seemed completely oblivious of this.

"What do you think?" Maggie asked Cari.

"I think we are all in serious trouble."

"Wow, thanks. That was super encouraging."

"Well, you don't know these men. I've seen the damage they can do."

"OK, let's think about this," Galen said, gently pushing one of his children back onto the pew. "They were elected by the membership right? So let's un-elect them. Let's vote for new elders. I don't care if they have to be people who live here. We can do better than this."

Cari groaned.

"What?" Galen said.

"Well, you see, Dan wasn't big on membership. So once these clowns took off, he never really made people jump through the hoops of membership. I mean, can you imagine asking Tiny to fill out a membership application? So we don't even have any members, according to the bylaws. I'm not even a member."

"But you were here back then, when all of the yogurt hit the fan?" Galen asked.

"Yes. Sort of. I was one of the first people Dan let stay here, but I was too caught up in my own issues to really care about church politics. I just knew that a lot of people were leaving, and fast. But I also didn't care. At the time, I didn't care about anything."

"That's hard to imagine," Maggie said.

"I know," Cari said. "It's hard to remember too."

"So what are we going to do?" Galen asked.

Maggie put her hand over his.

"I don't know," Cari said. "For now, I guess we pray. I mean, God must have a plan, right?"

Chapter 3

Though the elders had been busy hiring a new pastor, they'd also found time to obtain a pulpit. It was enormous and looked to be made of solid oak. "How'd they even get that thing in here?" Galen muttered to his wife.

"Crane, maybe?" she whispered back.

After a bewildered worship team led a few songs, Christian took the stage and his place behind the pulpit.

"He looks like a really small Jack in a really big box," Maggie whispered.

Galen gave her a scolding look.

"What? You started it!"

Pastor Chris introduced himself to the congregation. "Good morning, brothers and sisters. My name is Christian Hatch, and I am honored to serve as your new pastor. I know Pastor Dan left some big shoes to fill, and I'm not even going to try. But I will give you my best, and together I know we can accomplish great things."

The room was silent.

There were just over fifty people in attendance that morning, and about forty of them were living at the church. A few, like Galen's family, were regular attendees. Some might call them members, but they had never filled out any forms.

Pastor Chris spent most of his pulpit-time sharing about his background, paying particular attention to his bachelor's degree in

Bible studies and his Master of Divinity. The men stared straight ahead, the women played with their phones, and the children squirmed in their seats. But they were quiet at least. Finally, he wrapped up with a quick sermon on the seventy weeks of Daniel.

"What is he thinking with this?" Maggie whispered to Galen.

Galen didn't answer.

Daniel, who was sitting on the other side of Maggie's son, did answer her. "He's showing us how smart he is."

Maggie gave an apologetic glance to Harmony, as if to say she hadn't meant to be critical in front of Daniel. Harmony just shrugged, as if that was the least of their worries.

The lengthy service did finally end, and folks filed down the stairs to lunch. As Galen and Maggie made their way to the door, Pastor Chris beckoned to Maggie from the office. Maggie looked at Galen. "We'll be waiting in the car," he said, and continued toward the door.

Maggie dragged her feet into the office. "Yes?"

"Would you please go get me some lunch?"

"What?"

"I've got some calls to make," he said, and pointed toward Pastor Dan's office with this chin, "so I'd like to eat in my office."

"OK, but why would you ask me to go get you lunch? Why can't you get it yourself?"

Pastor Chris looked sincerely surprised. "I'm sorry. I thought you were the pastor's secretary."

"Um, no. I volunteer to run the office, like, for the homeless people. But I don't wait on the pastor."

Chris chuckled, but it came out awkwardly. "OK, well, you do live here, right?"

Maggie looked toward the door, as if hoping Galen would reappear to rescue her. "No, I don't live here. But wait, so you're saying, if I did live here, then I would be compelled, out of like gratitude or something, to go get your lunch?"

"No, that's not what I was saying at all. I just thought you were a resident."

"Guest."

"Beg your pardon?"

"We call them guests here."

"Oh, right. Guests. Well, then, have a good day. I'm sorry about the misunderstanding."

Maggie practically ran out of the office. When she got to the car, she was out of breath.

"What was that all about?"

"He wanted me to fetch him his lunch."

"Seriously?" Galen started to climb back out of the car.

"What are you doing?"

"I'm going to go give him a piece of my mind."

"No, never mind. It's over. Let's just go home. I need a nap."

Galen started the car and pulled out of the parking lot.

"Are we going to go to a different church now?" Isaiah piped up from the backseat.

Galen and Maggie exchanged a look. "Why would you ask that, buddy?" Galen asked.

"Daniel said that we would probably go to a different church now. He said that everyone would except for the homeless people."

"I don't know, buddy," Galen said.

Maggie quickly added, "No. We are not abandoning our church." Then she looked at her husband sternly. "Not to toot our own horns, but the whole place would fall apart without us, and you know that."

"Well then," Galen muttered, muffling his voice for backseat ears, "maybe then they'd appreciate you."

"Is that what this is really about? Is that why we serve there?"

Galen sighed. "Once again, my own words coming back to bite me."

"He's not eating with us," Daniel said.

Harmony looked around as if to confirm his observation. "No, none of them are."

"Pastor Dan always ate with us."

"I know, honey."

Daniel was quiet for a few minutes, apparently lost in thought.

"Finish your lunch, honey, and then we can go for a walk or something."

Daniel looked at his mom. "I don't think anyone knows how much trouble we're in."

She rolled her eyes. "Don't be so dramatic. Eat your cauliflower."

Daniel scrunched up his nose and pushed his plate away from him. "I'm fasting."

"Fine," Harmony said, obviously annoyed. She stood up, grabbed both their trays and headed toward the tray return. She scraped the plates off, put them in the bin, and then turned back toward where she'd left her son sitting.

He was gone.

"Oh, good grief," she muttered. She looked around the kitchen, but didn't see any clues as to his whereabouts. She climbed the stairs and went back into the sanctuary, where she found him, alone, kneeling at the altar, his little hands folded into a ball and his head bowed. She tiptoed up behind him and laid a hand on his small shoulder. "I'll be in our room. Come find me when you're done."

Harmony and Daniel shared a room with another mother and son team—Jessica and her two-year-old Jayden. When Harmony got back to her room, Jessica was sitting on the edge of Jayden's bed, looking sick with worry.

"What's wrong?" Harmony asked.

"I can't get him to wake up. He said he didn't feel good this morning. Then he fell asleep during that awful preaching. I couldn't get him to wake up so I carried him in here, but I'm starting to get worried."

Harmony looked down at the toddler, who was breathing fast and hard. "Has he got a fever?" Harmony reached down and touched the little boy's head. Then she yanked her hand away. "Yeah, he's burning up. I'll go get Pastor D…" She looked at Jessica. "I don't know who to get. Maggie's not here. She went home."

"Should we call an ambulance?" Jessica asked in a shaky voice.

Daniel appeared in the doorway. "What's going on?" he asked. Both women ignored him. "Is Jayden sick?" Both women ignored him again. Daniel walked over to where Jayden lay, and Harmony gently pushed him away.

"Give him some space, honey," she said to Daniel. Then, to Jessica, "Yeah, I would call 911."

"OK," Jessica said as she got up to get the phone.

Daniel knelt beside his young friend and gently placed his hand on his forehead. Then he said, "God, please heal Jayden. In Jesus' name, amen."

Immediately, Jayden's little eyelids fluttered, and then he opened his eyes and looked up at the three faces peering down at him. "Mama?"

"I'm right here, baby." Jessica sat back down on the bed, and Jayden scrambled up into her arms. She kissed him on the forehead. Then she looked at Daniel wide-eyed. "How did you do that?"

"I didn't do anything," Daniel said. Then he crawled up onto his top bunk and opened his Bible.

"That's some kid you've got there," Jessica said.

Harmony looked pale. It took several seconds for her to answer Jessica. Finally, she stammered, "Well, yes he is, but I really don't think he did anything here. I mean, Daniel is no miracle worker. It's just a coincidence. You were just feeling better, weren't you, Jayden?" She reached out and squeezed his foot.

Jayden didn't answer her. He just stuck his thumb in his mouth and pushed his head deeper into his mother's chest.

Two things travel really fast in a homeless shelter: viruses and gossip. By supper, everyone had heard about Jayden's recovery. Natalia was the first to approach Daniel. His fast apparently over, he was biting into a sloppy joe when Natalia asked him if he could lay hands on her lower back. Then George (who demanded people call him "Chief" because he was, he claimed, from Kansas City) physically pushed Natalia and her measly back pain to the side and put both hands on the table, leaned in so he was eye level with Daniel, and said, "I have gout in my big toe."

Predictably, Daniel shrank back at the sight of him, and Harmony sprang into mama bear mode. "Get out of here, both of you. He doesn't have any healing powers. He's just a kid."

Not looking convinced, Chief did slink away. But most of the diners kept an eye on Daniel throughout the meal.

Chapter 4

Galen had his head under an F150 hood when his garage phone rang. Wiping his hands along the way, he walked into his small office to sit down and take the call.

"G's Automotives?" he answered.

"Hey, G? This is Pete."

"Hey, Pete, how's it going?"

"Not good, as a matter of fact. Hey listen, I was supposed to do Bible study tonight, but Pastor Chris says I can't. He says us *residents* can't teach anymore. I really wasn't planning on teaching or anything, just reading and praying, but whatever. Can you fill in for me?"

Galen paused.

"You there?"

"Yeah ... um ... did Chris say he wanted me to do it?"

"No, but who else is there? You're the only non-homeless person who does Bible study, except for Pastor Dan, and I doubt he's available."

Galen sighed. "Yeah, sure. I can do it tonight, but I'm not sure how this is going to pan out. I don't want to do Bible study every night, and I don't think you guys want to listen to me that often either."

"Hey, man, now that we get to listen to Pastor Chris, we'll take anything else."

Galen stifled a laugh. "OK then, thanks for the call. I'll see you in a few hours."

Galen went to church early to fill Maggie in.

He peeked into the office. No Maggie. He followed the winding hallways to the other end of the building, to the church's hair salon.

His sons—who always got off the bus at the church, along with Daniel and any other child who happened to be staying there at the time—were playing with tablets in the hallway outside of the salon. "Hey, kids. Is your mom in here?"

Without looking up from his game, Isaiah nodded.

Galen walked into the salon and found his wife happily snipping away at someone's hair.

She looked up when he walked in. "Good afternoon. I'm a bit busy right now, sir, but if you'll have a seat in the waiting area, I'll see if I can fit you in."

Galen smiled. "Don't need a trim. Just wanted to tell you that I'm doing Bible study tonight. You and the boys don't have to stick around if you don't want to, but I wanted to keep you in the loop." As he spoke, he did have a seat in the waiting area, which was just a well-worn couch against the wall. He propped his feet up on the also-well-worn coffee table, which was adorned with several magazines.

Maggie frowned. "Yeah, I heard about that. Well, not about you doing it. But about the new rule."

"What new rule?" the woman in the chair asked.

Maggie said, "Well, the new pastor doesn't want people who are staying here to lead Bible study. I guess he wants them to be ministered *to* more than to be minister*ing*."

"Oh, well, that's stupid. I like it when Pete does Bible study."

"I think you're done," Maggie said. She removed the cape and shook it off.

The woman stood up and stretched. She looked in the mirror and fluffed her hair. "Thank you. It looks so much better!"

"You bet," Maggie said.

The woman dropped a few coins into Maggie's tip jar and then bounced out of the salon.

"Another happy customer, I see," Galen said.

"Yeah, that's Brandy. She comes in about once a week." Maggie chuckled. "But I don't mind. She's nice. I think she just wants someone to talk to. So, you going to do Bible study every night now?"

"No. I was thinking about asking some of the others to take a night or two. I'm assuming you don't want to do it. But I could ask Roger or Mike."

Maggie grimaced.

"What?" Galen asked.

"Sadie told me today that she and Roger are thinking about leaving the church." She picked up a broom and started sweeping up hair.

"Already?" Galen asked. "It's only been one Sunday. Let's give the guy a chance."

"It's not him," Maggie said. She glanced at the door. "I don't mean to gossip, but apparently they know Phil somehow, and they said they want to stay far away from him. They advised us to do the same."

"Well, isn't that handy?" Galen got up to leave.

"We'll stay for Bible study," Maggie said as Galen left the room and made his way back to the sanctuary. He met several people along the way and greeted each of them with a smile, calling them by name.

Tiny took one look at him and asked, "You OK, G?"

Galen's mouth smiled, but his eyes didn't. "Sure am. God is good!" he said and continued on.

Before he could turn into the sanctuary, Pastor Chris spotted him and called out, "Could I speak to you for a minute, Mr. Turney?"

Galen groaned quietly and then obliged.

Chris nodded at the door. "Go ahead and shut it, would you?"

Galen did.

"Thanks. Have a seat."

Galen sat. "Already got some new furniture, I see?" Galen asked.

"Well, yes. Truth be told, I was scared to sit in some of the old stuff. Afraid it would crumble beneath me. Don't have time for a broken tailbone!" Chris laughed loudly.

Galen's mouth smiled again.

"So, I have a proposition for you," Chris said. "Thank you for volunteering to cover Bible study tonight. The elders and I have talked, and we don't think we should have residents doing the teaching. They are here to get back on their feet and don't need to be spending their energy trying to lead others when they're not even able to lead themselves. We also don't think anyone who isn't a church member should be teaching—"

"I'm not a church member," Galen interrupted.

"Yes, well, we're hoping you'll consider that. I have an application right here for you." Chris patted a manila folder on his desk. "It's just a few questions. Just a formality really."

"A formality," Galen said. He rubbed his jaw with one hand, as if he was processing something complicated. "So then what, the elders vote on whether or not I'm good enough to be a member?"

Chris laughed. "No, no, nothing like that. We vote, yes, but not about whether or not you're good enough. We just vote on whether you're someone we want to be part of the body here, which I'm sure you are."

Galen was quiet, still rubbing his jaw.

"So the proposition is this. If you will become a member, we would like to offer you a paying position of Bible study leader. You would lead Bible study every weeknight, and I would take care of Saturday nights and Sunday mornings."

Galen didn't answer.

Pastor Chris gave him about three seconds and then asked, "Well?"

"I'll have to pray about it," Galen said, standing up. He turned to leave the office.

"Don't forget your paperwork," the pastor said, holding out the manila folder.

Galen turned back and took the outstretched folder. He nodded, but even his mouth didn't smile this time.

Late that night, Galen sat alone at his kitchen table, his head in his hands, his eyes staring down at his Bible, which was open to Revelation.

Maggie soundlessly came into the kitchen and laid a hand on his back. "Doing some light reading, I see. Are you ever going to come to bed?"

"Yeah, I'm just trying to make up my mind or I'll never fall asleep."

Maggie sat down across from him. "Do you want to talk about it?"

Galen shook his head, not looking up. "No, thanks. I just wish God would make it clear to me what I'm supposed to do."

"I understand. OK then." She got back up, kissed him on top of his head and said, "I love you. Whatever you and God decide, I am sure it will be right."

He looked up then. "What if I did it but said no to the paycheck?"

"Yeah, OK."

"Really?"

"Yeah, of course."

"Are you sure? I mean, it would be *every* night. That's a lot of time away from home."

"So we'll go to Bible study too. The kids will love it. If you remember, there was a time when I went to an Open Door Bible study every night."

Galen smiled then, with both his mouth and his eyes. He gave his wife a long kiss. "I do remember. OK then. Let's do it for a while and see how it goes. But I'm not filling out any membership forms and I'm not taking any money from a homeless shelter."

Chapter 5

The following Sunday, it was almost business as usual. A few of the church's guests had moved on, including the three-generational family who had just moved in, and a few new people had arrived and were settling in.

One of the newcomers was Dwight Schultz. He had shared with Maggie that he was an Iraq veteran, and he certainly looked the part. He was tall, muscular, and clean-cut. And on Sunday morning, there he was sitting right up front.

Pastor Chris preached on the Fall, and some of the people appeared to be listening. Some of those appeared to be understanding. His rhetoric was still a bit lofty for them, but he was improving.

Maggie leaned over and whispered to Galen, "Sadie and Roger aren't here."

"I noticed."

"Neither's Cari," Maggie added.

"I know."

"Mike and Lisa are here though."

"Good. And we've still got Sally and Gertrude."

Maggie stifled a giggle. "Sally's not here," she whispered. "I should probably check on her, make sure she's OK." Maggie glanced around the sanctuary. "And I haven't seen Gertrude in weeks now that you mention it."

"She's probably off fighting crime. She'll be back."

Maggie giggled aloud, and Pastor Chris gave her a stern look. She quickly bowed her head and hid her face. "And, of course, the elders are here."

"Right, the elders."

At the end of the service, Pastor Chris gave an eloquent altar call, and Joyce, a woman who had also joined them in the past week, went down front and knelt in front of the altar.

Daniel looked up at his mother. "Can I go?"

Harmony looked surprised, but nodded and stepped back so her son could pass.

He slowly but purposefully made his way to the altar. Then he knelt beside the woman. He looked up at her with wide, blue eyes and whispered, "Does it hurt?"

Her teary eyes widened at his question, and she nodded.

Daniel smiled and placed his small hand on the back of her neck. Then he closed his eyes and prayed.

After the service, Pastor Chris asked Galen into his office.

"This is getting to be a routine," Galen said.

"I know. Have a seat?"

Galen sat.

"So, I've learned that you used to be on the worship team."

"Yes, several years ago. I haven't played much—"

Chris interrupted him. "We really need someone to take over the music on Saturday nights, and especially Sunday mornings."

"Why?" Galen asked with a distinct lack of couth.

"Well, the elders and I, we just don't think it's appropriate to have the homeless leading worship. Once again, they are here to learn, not to lead."

"But Pastor, these people are talented musicians and they love to play. I mean, I think they *are* learning. They are learning through doing."

"I understand your position, but I still don't think it looks good to have these people up front."

Galen stood. "I'm sorry, but I can't lead Bible study Monday through Friday and then lead worship Saturday and Sunday."

"The offer of a paid position still stands," Chris said as Galen left the office.

As Galen and Chris were talking, an ecstatic Joyce was gushing to Harmony, "I don't know how he did it. I mean, I've had this pain for two weeks. Even went to the emergency room, but they only gave me Advil and sent me away. But your son, he healed me. I mean, he really healed me! The pain is completely gone. I can't believe it. How did he do that?"

Harmony looked dumbfounded.

Daniel spoke up. "I didn't do anything. It wasn't me. It was God. And please don't tell anyone. Come on, Mama," he said, pulling on Harmony's hand. "I'm hungry."

Joyce followed Harmony and Daniel to lunch. She sat alone and ate quietly, seeming to enjoy her newfound pain-free condition. She told no one about what had happened. But when she got back to her room, she posted about her miracle on Facebook. She gave all the glory to God, and mentioned that her healing had come at the hands of a young boy named Daniel.

On Wednesday, Maggie helped a young woman named Annette get settled in to one of the family rooms. The church didn't always have as many cribs as babies, but this time they did have one for Annette's ten-month-old daughter, Emma. Annette placed Emma into the crib and then collapsed on the bed. "Thank you so much," she said to Maggie. "I don't know what we would have done if it weren't for this place. We'd be sleeping outside." She paused for a second, and then added, "We don't even have a car to sleep in."

"No problem," Maggie said. "That's why we're here, and the more cute little ones like this, the better." Maggie rubbed one of Emma's chubby little hands, which were white-knuckling the edge of the crib. "You let me know if you need anything. I'll either be in the office or at the other end of the church, in the hair salon. And we'll see you tonight at Bible study."

"And that's like mandatory, right?" Annette asked.

"Yes, we do ask our guests to attend a Bible study every night. It's really our only rule. Well, that, and there's no drugs or alcohol allowed."

"What about smoking?"

"Good question. You can't smoke in the church, but people have set up some lawn chairs across the parking lot. They smoke over there, and so far, no one has complained."

"OK, great. Thanks," Annette said and lay down.

Maggie spent the afternoon in the salon. Several people needed trims, one woman came in from town for a color, and Dwight Schultz wanted a touch-up on his crewcut.

When Galen got there, Maggie was just cleaning up. She collapsed on the couch beside him. "I'm pooped."

"Busy day?"

"Yeah, only one new guest, but the salon has been hopping all afternoon."

Galen put his arm around her and pulled her close. "Any new crisis I should be aware of?"

Maggie hesitated.

"What? There is one?"

"Well no, it's not a crisis exactly. It's just, well, I hesitate to even say anything."

"Since when?" Galen said and then laughed.

Maggie playfully punched him in the side. "You hush. Well, you know how women have like a sixth sense about creepozoids?"

"Yeah?"

"Well, I'm not accusing him of anything, but that new guy Dwight, there was just something off about him. I mean, he didn't even do anything, but I was *not* comfortable being alone with him."

"You mean the veteran?"

"Yes. Sorry to speak ill of him. He's probably perfectly fine."

"No, not necessarily. Chris told me that Dwight has a pretty bad case of PTSD, so maybe you just sensed that he's not at peace right now."

"Is a pastor supposed to be telling you stuff like that?"

"Maybe. He was telling me in the context of what to talk about in Bible study. But I probably shouldn't have told *you*, so mum's the word, OK?"

"OK."

"Should we get Harmony to stay in here with you? Like the old days when you used to give haircuts in the men's bathroom?"

Maggie laughed and punched him lightly in the side again. "I never cut any hair in the *men's* bathroom. It was the women's bathroom. And I'm not sure Harmony would love that."

"Why, what does she do all day?"

"Not much. You know what? I think it might be a better job for Tiny. He's usually covering the office when I'm down here, but we could probably find someone else to take his place."

"Well, if you can take that much Tiny, then by all means. Put his adoration to good use. Come on, let's go to Bible study. The boys are probably already in there."

The boys weren't the only ones. There were several new faces in the sanctuary. "Do you know these people?" Galen muttered.

"No. Tiny was in the office, and he's supposed to come get me if someone new arrives. I'll find out." Maggie approached an older couple sitting near the back. They were well-dressed, but Maggie had learned that didn't necessarily mean they weren't in need of a roof for the night. "Good evening," she said, extending her hand. The man shook it. "My name is Maggie." She sat down in the pew in front of them. "Welcome to Open Door Church."

"Thank you. I'm Russ, and this is my wife Irene."

"Pleasure to meet you," Maggie said. "Do you need a place to stay tonight?"

"Oh no," the man said, as if that was absurd. "We're just visiting. Your website said that your services are open to the public. Is that not true?"

"That is absolutely true. We just don't usually get a lot of visitors on weeknights, and truth be told, I don't think anyone has updated that website in years. I'd almost forgotten about it altogether!"

"Oh really? It looked very up-to-date yesterday. Had a picture of your new pastor and everything."

"Oh, sorry. I didn't realize someone had done that! Well, the new pastor probably won't be here tonight."

"Oh, that's all right. We're actually here to see the child. Can you point him out?"

Maggie was flummoxed. "The child?"

"Yes, the one who heals? Irene here has lung cancer."

Maggie gasped. After a few awkward seconds, she said, "I'm so sorry to hear that. Excuse me for just a second." She stood up and practically ran to Galen, who was talking to Pete up front. "Sorry, Pete. I need him for a sec." She grabbed Galen's arm and pulled him to the side.

"What?" he asked, alarmed.

"The older couple, in the back. Don't look."

Galen looked. "Yeah?"

"They are here because of Daniel. The woman has cancer. They want him to heal her."

"They said that?"

"Pretty much," Maggie said, crossing her arms in front of her chest as if she'd suddenly caught a chill.

"Is that why the other new people are here too?"

"I don't know. What are we going to do? It's not like Daniel can cure cancer!"

"I have no idea. I guess we should talk to Daniel," Galen said.

38

"You mean Harmony, right? Daniel's only eight."

"OK, let's talk to them both." Galen glanced at the clock and then, though it was time to start, went and sat down in front of Harmony and Daniel.

"What's up, G?" Harmony asked. "You look tense."

"Well, I think that there are some people here tonight to see Daniel." Daniel looked around. Harmony didn't. She just stared at Galen. "They seem to think he can heal them. I'm not sure how you want to handle it."

"Can I talk to them?" Daniel asked.

Galen looked at Harmony, who shrugged. "I guess so, little buddy," Galen said.

Daniel got up and headed toward the front of the sanctuary.

"I thought he meant go talk to them privately," Galen whispered to Harmony.

"Excuse me," Daniel said from the front. The room quieted down instantly, which was a miracle in itself. "My name is Daniel, and I have prayed for some people, and then God has healed them. But I want you to know that I don't have some sort of Superman power or anything. I'm just a kid. If you are here tonight, I will pray for you. But I don't know if God will heal you. Sometimes I feel like I just have to pray for someone. Then I do. But right now I'm not feeling that." Immediately after speaking, Daniel returned to his seat. The sanctuary remained silent.

Galen took this as his cue and went up front. "Welcome to Open Door, folks. It's nice to see we have some new faces joining us this evening. I'm just going to read and talk about a short Scripture, and then I'll invite anyone who would like to, to come on down to the altar for prayer, OK? For now, let's begin with a prayer." He cleared his throat nervously. He usually asked someone else to do the praying aloud part for him, as he really didn't like doing it. But this time, he seemed to be up for the challenge. "Father," he said and then took a deep breath, "I thank you for bringing these people here to gather in your name. I ask you to take control of this service, to take control of this church, of this building and this body of believers, and I ask that your will be done. I know there are people here who are hurting, physically, emotionally, spiritually, and I ask that you heal each and every one of them." Someone near the front snickered, which was unusual; snickers usually came from the back. "I ask you to bless our time here, and give me the words you want me to say. In Jesus' name I pray, amen." Galen raised his head and leveled his gaze in the direction whence the snicker had come and found himself making eye contact with Dwight Schultz.

Chapter 6

"I don't think he healed anyone."

"I know, Tiny," Maggie said. "But maybe God *did* heal someone. We wouldn't necessarily know it happened."

"Yeah, but the kid prayed for a *lot* of people last night. And I didn't see anything change."

It was Thursday morning, and Maggie was only on her second cup of coffee. She was ordering supplies for the salon and seemed to be working fairly hard at not being annoyed with Tiny as he processed the events of the night before. Her efforts seemed to be failing as she slapped the desk and shouted, "Ah, crud!"

Tiny jumped. "What's wrong?"

"Nothing. I'll be right back. Would you please make some more coffee, Tiny?"

She got up and knocked on Pastor Chris's door.

"Yes?"

She walked in. "The church's credit card isn't working. Did you do something?"

He smiled. "Yes, sorry, we canceled that account as we weren't sure who had cards."

"There's only one card, and it stays in the safe."

"Well, now all orders are going to go through our treasurer."

"Phil?"

"Yes, Phil."

"So Phil wants to deal with salon supplies?" Maggie said with no little snark.

"Mrs. Turney, why don't you shut the door and have a seat?" Chris said, leaning back in his ergonomic chair. Maggie did as she was asked. "I've been meaning to ask you about the salon."

"OK?" Maggie said, defensively.

"Can you tell me exactly how that works?"

"Sure. What do you want to know?"

"Well, the supplies go on the church credit card?"

"Yes," Maggie said. "At first. I only order if there's enough money in the safe to pay for it. We don't go in debt over conditioner, but I use the credit card so I can order online, yes."

"OK, but the church is paying for the supplies?"

"Right."

"And how much do you charge?"

"I don't charge anything. Some people pay what they can, but most people can't pay. It's a ministry, not a business, and it's been working just fine for almost ten years."

"OK, OK," Chris said, holding his hands up. "I was just curious. We're just going to try to keep a better account of what's coming in and going out, that's all. So yes, make a list of what you need, and let Phil know."

Maggie sighed. "OK," she said, and stood up to go.

"Wait just a sec, if you will."

"Yeah?" She turned back around, but didn't sit.

"We've got some people coming in to update our audio visual room this afternoon. So can you make yourself available to help if they need it?"

"Yeah, why, where are you going to be?"

"I've got a meeting to get to here soon." He glanced at his watch. "And I probably won't be back."

"OK, so I just need to show them the sound booth?"

"Right. And just stick around if they need anything else. You know, sort of act like a buffer between them and the residents if you can."

Maggie folded her arms across her chest. "Wow."

Pastor Chris didn't seem to notice her disgust. "Thanks a lot," he said in a tone that said she was dismissed.

She left his office, closing the door behind her harder than she needed to. Tiny was sitting at her desk, playing with her stapler.

"What's wrong?" Tiny asked.

"Nothing," Maggie lied.

"What did Pastor want?"

"He said we have some people coming in today to update the sound room. He wanted me to know."

"Oh." Tiny got out of her chair and sat down in his. "What's wrong with our sound room?"

"No idea, but would you do me a favor, Tiny? I'll be in the salon this afternoon. And I know I asked you to hang out with me down there, but could you also check in on the sound room every few minutes, just to make sure they're doing OK?"

"Yeah. I can do that, Maggie."

They weren't just updating the sound room—they were *gutting* it. They filled the dumpster outside and they carried in load after load of shiny electronics. Tiny did end up being a help with the lugging, and the men didn't seem to mind their lack of a buffer one bit.

At one point, Maggie let out a low whistle. "This must have cost a fortune," she said to one of the men.

"Well, yes, but don't worry. Most of it is just on loan from JCTV."

"JCTV? Why?"

"Oh, I figured you knew. You guys have a contract with them now. They're going to air your Saturday and Sunday services, starting this Sunday."

Maggie laughed. "Seriously? Have they *seen* one of our services? This isn't exactly Lakewood, you know."

The man shrugged and walked away. He didn't seem to know or care what Lakewood was.

"What's Lakewood?" Tiny asked, out of breath from all his exertions.

"It's a giant church in Texas. Their services are on TV."

"Oh. Is that the church that paid for our addition?"

"No, same city, but different church. Apparently, there's lots of churches in Houston."

"Oh. So why did you say we weren't Lakewood? Of course we're not Lakewood. We're not in Texas. I've never been to Texas."

"I know, Tiny. I said that just because I think it's a little funny that we're going to be on TV, that's all."

"We're going to be on TV?" Tiny said, elated. "That's awesome! Can you give me a haircut first?"

Sure enough, on Sunday morning, JCTV did send a few people to film the service.

"Unbelievable," Maggie said to Galen, halfway through the service.

"What?"

"Everyone is on their best behavior. It's like someone cast a television spell."

"What, did you want them to act out?"

"Yeah, actually. I did. I wanted them to embarrass Chris."

"Maggie!" Galen half-scolded her. "Stop it!"

She smiled mischievously. "Sorry, just telling the truth."

At the end of the service, Chris gave a moving altar call and several people went down front, including Dwight, who appeared to be wearing new jeans and a new button-up shirt. After the music stopped, Chris asked Dwight to stand beside him. Chris put his arm around Dwight's wide shoulders and said, "I'd like to introduce you all to Dwight here."

"Geesh," Galen muttered. "Hope the guy doesn't mind being in the spotlight."

"Dwight," Chris continued, "is a war hero. He served two tours in Iraq, and like so many of our country's veterans, came home to homelessness. We are honored to have him staying here with us, and we thank God that today, Dwight has chosen to give his heart to Jesus."

Chris began to applaud then, and some followed suit, but they looked confused as they did so.

People weren't used to cheering after altar calls.

The next morning, the safe had been taken out of the office. As soon as Maggie saw Pastor Chris, she asked, "I assume someone official removed the safe, and that we haven't been robbed by someone with a forklift?"

Chris chuckled. "Yes, we took it out. We won't actually be storing any money at the church anymore. You've got enough to do without worrying about finances."

"OK," Maggie said and turned to go. Then she thought better of it. "And I've been meaning to ask. Are you going to move into the parsonage?"

"No," Chris answered quickly. "It's a nice thought, but I have a house, where I live with my wife."

Maggie looked surprised. She had never seen hide nor hair of a wife. She slyly glanced at his left hand, and sure enough, there was a ring there. "Oh. Do you have any ideas about what to do with it?"

"Not at this point, no."

"OK, well, sometimes, especially in winter, we do fill up around here. Maybe we could convert it to more rooms?"

"Maybe," Chris said, but he walked away before Maggie could say anything else.

When Maggie got back to the office, Annette was waiting for her, holding baby Emma on one hip. "Hi, Annette! Have a seat!" Annette looked at Tiny nervously, so Maggie pulled one of the chairs over closer to her own. "What can I do for you?" Maggie asked.

"Um, I was wondering if I could talk to the pastor?"

"Oh, of course. I was just talking to him. But I'm not sure where he was headed. Let me give him a call." Maggie dialed his cell.

"Yes?"

"Hi, Pastor. We have someone here who needs to talk to you?"

"Who?"

"Annette."

There was a short pause. "Is she a resident?"

"Yup."

"All right ... well ... do you know what she needs?"

"Nope."

"Well, can you ask?"

"Nope."

"OK, tell her I'll be back this afternoon. I've got a meeting right now."

"OK." Maggie hung up the phone. "I'm sorry, Annette, he's in a meeting I guess. He said he'd be back this afternoon. Is there anything I can help you with?"

"No," Annette said sheepishly. "I'll just wait."

"OK, well, let me know if you need anything," Maggie said.

She left the office, but was still within earshot when Tiny said, "Pastor Dan always talked to us."

"I know, Tiny."

"He liked talking to us."

"I know, Tiny. He really did."

When afternoon came, Annette and her baby found Maggie and Tiny in the salon. Maggie was giving Sally a perm. Sally didn't have much hair left to curl, but Maggie had been practicing on her for years, so she was a pro. She looked up at Annette as her hands kept working.

"Hey, Annette!" she said brightly.

"Hey, um, I was looking for the pastor? He's still not in his office. Do you know if he's back?"

"I don't know. Would you like to come in and have a seat? Tiny, would you mind doing a round and see if you can find Pastor? If you can't, I'll give him another call."

Tiny grunted as he got up and left without a word. Annette took his seat.

"I think little Emma has grown in just these few days," Maggie said.

"Well, she sure does eat," Annette said. She was looking at her daughter with adoration, but her voice sounded tired.

After a few minutes, Tiny returned. "I don't think he's here. His car isn't in the parking lot either."

"OK, hang on just a sec, and I'll call," Maggie said.

Tiny sat down next to Annette on the couch. Annette looked uncomfortable, but she also looked too tired to move.

"You getting any sleep here?" Maggie asked Annette.

She looked up at Maggie as if she were guilty of something. "No, not really. Sorry, it's not a bad place or anything. I just can't seem to shut my brain off so I can go to sleep."

Maggie nodded. "I understand that! OK, Sally, this is the last curl." She snapped the last rod into place. "Sit tight. I'll be right back."

"Getting too old to move anyhow," Sally said with a giggle that made her sound much younger than she was.

Maggie pawed through her crowded counter until she came up with her phone. She stabbed at the screen and then held the phone to her ear. "Sorry, he's not answering," she said to Annette. "Do you want me to leave a message?"

Annette shook her head. "No, that's OK. Can you just check me out?"

Maggie looked surprised. "Of course. Do you have somewhere else to go?"

Annette didn't answer.

"Sweetie, what's wrong?"

"Nothing," Annette said. "It's OK. We just need to go." But the tears in her eyes said it was not OK.

"OK, then come with me, please. Sorry, Sally. I'll be back for you." Sally didn't respond, but Sally's hearing wasn't the best anymore. Maggie put an arm around Annette's shoulders and led her out of the salon. There really was no formal checkout process, so Maggie led Annette back to her room. She sat down on the edge of Annette's bed and patted the spot beside her. Annette sat down, but kept her eyes pointed down at her hands.

"Talk to me, Annette. What's going on?"

"It's no big deal. Really. I just ... we'll just find somewhere else to go. I mean, I'm homeless, but that doesn't mean that I need to put up with bullies. We'll figure it out."

"Bullies?" Maggie said. She hadn't heard that word used in their church before. "What happened?"

"Really, it's no big deal. But I'm just not going to stay here."

"But who was a bully to you?"

"I'm not a rat," Annette said and stood up.

"Of course not, but maybe we can fix it. No one should be bullying you. You should be safe here."

"What do I need to do to check out?"

"You don't need to do anything. You can leave whenever you want."

"OK," Annette said, picking up a bag that was apparently all packed.

"But Annette," Maggie tried, "please don't go. We can work this out. Give me a chance to fix things. My husband can probably talk to whoever it is who's bothering you—"

"Don't worry about it. We'll be OK. I didn't really want to stay in a church anyway." She picked up Emma, gave a glance around the small room, and then headed for the door.

"You can also come back whenever you want," Maggie said, but Annette just kept walking.

Chapter 7

After her little chat with Annette, Maggie began to watch the church guests like a hawk.

At Bible study that night, Galen asked her, "What's got you in a tizzy?"

She told him about Annette. He didn't seem as shook up as she was, and she let him know that this was unacceptable.

"What do you want me to say?" Galen asked.

"Never mind. You've obviously never been homeless," Maggie snapped.

"Seriously?" Galen asked, and headed up front.

As she watched him walk away, she witnessed a bizarre interaction. Melanie was sitting in the aisle seat of the front pew. She was the only one sitting in the front pew. Yet Chief walked up to her, hit her in the shoulder with his Bible and barked, "This is my seat." She jumped up like a scared rabbit and moved a full two rows back. Galen, having missed the exchange, called everyone to prayer. As he prayed, Maggie continued to survey the congregation, wondering if Chief was in fact the mystery bully. She didn't see anyone else beating any brows. Most people had their eyes closed and their heads bowed. But as her gaze swept toward the back, she made eye contact with Dwight, whose eyes were wide open and ablaze with something that looked a lot like hatred. Instinctively, her head snapped front and down, and she squeezed her eyes shut—the little hairs on the back of her neck now very much at attention.

To his credit, Galen focused his message on bullying, looking at Matthew 7:12, Mark 12:31, and Romans 12:18.

After the closing prayer, Maggie turned to Harmony. "Can I ask you something?"

"Shoot."

"Is there anyone living here who you would classify as a bully?"

"You mean Chief?"

"That didn't take you long to think of him."

"Well, the guy's a dry drunk. And a jerk."

"Harmony! Keep your voice down!"

"You brought it up!"

"So what's he do exactly? And why don't I know about it?"

"I dunno. He's just a real grouch. He's been here so long he thinks he owns the place. And he's gotten much worse since Dan died. I think he's grieving or something. Anyway, I stay away from him. And I keep Daniel away from him, but the guys who live with him? Those guys need prayer."

"Huh. So what do you think we should do about it?"

"No idea. I mean, Pastor Dan knew about it, and he was trying to counsel Chief through it, but now … he's like a really mean sheep with no shepherd."

After Galen and Maggie got the kids into bed, Maggie tried again. "Harmony says Chief is the issue."

"I'm not surprised. He's not the most pleasant individual. I've seen him throw his weight around. But that Dwight guy is no picnic either."

"Well, at least he's a new Christian. Chief has been going to daily Bible studies for three years, at least."

"I think it's closer to five," Galen said. "Can we talk about something else?"

"Why?"

"Because I live and breathe that shelter. Now I just want to go to bed in my own home. I just want to think about something else. Want to watch a movie?"

"Sure. Can I ask you just one more thing?"

Galen sighed. "Ahuh."

"Can you talk to him?"

"Who, Chief?"

"Yeah, Harmony says that Dan was counseling him. Maybe you could help."

"Honey, I don't know. Let me think about it, OK?"

"OK."

"And you just stay away from him."

The next morning, Maggie accosted Pastor Chris before he could even get into his office. "What happened to you yesterday?"

Chris didn't look at her. He just unlocked his door and went inside, saying, "I had a lot to do. What do you need?"

"Well, we had a young woman and her baby *leave* yesterday because she was being bullied, and you couldn't be bothered to help her with it."

Chris still didn't look at her. He made himself busy shuffling some paperwork around on his desk. "Bullied? Well, I'm not surprised. We're not exactly a country club."

"What is that supposed to mean?" Maggie put her hands on her hips, her face much redder than usual.

Finally, he looked at her. "You know exactly what I mean. We have homeless people here. They are not exactly the most sociable, the most refined folks. Of course we're going to have behavioral issues. Some of these people just got out of prison."

"Jail."

"What?"

"We don't have anyone who just got out of prison. They just got out of jail. There's a difference."

"Pardon my error." He looked down at his papers.

"And bullying is not normal around here. I've *never* heard of an issue before now. Sure, people are grumpy, but this girl used the word *bullies*. This was no small thing. She was actually scared to stay here."

"OK then. Thank you for telling me," Chris said dismissively.

"So, how do I reach you if there's an emergency? What if someone else wants to talk to you? What if it's about something more pressing than bullying? How am I supposed to get you?"

"You can text me," he said condescendingly. "I'll answer you when I'm able."

Later that week, two newcomers walked into the sanctuary about halfway through Galen's Bible study. One of the men wore sunglasses and carried a white cane. Galen did not pause, but did nod and smile at them in greeting. They sat near the back.

When Galen was about to close in prayer, he asked if there were any specific requests. One of the men stood up. "My friend here is blind. We've come in hopes the child Daniel would pray for him."

Maggie heard Harmony gasp. Galen looked at Harmony, but she didn't give him any indication of how to answer.

Daniel took the lead. He stood up, walked to the back of the sanctuary, and knelt in front of the blind man. He whispered to the man, so quietly only those closest to him could hear, "I don't know God's will for you, but I will pray." Then he bowed his head and muttered something unintelligible. It seemed the entire congregation was holding their breath. Daniel said, "In Jesus' name I pray, amen." The blind man bent and kissed Daniel on the head, and then Daniel stood, but still, the sanctuary was silent, as if everyone was waiting for the man to leap to his feet and say, "I can see!"

That did not happen.

Galen closed in prayer and then dismissed everyone. Maggie was going to stop and make sure the men did not need a place to stay, but by the time she weaved her way to the back of the sanctuary, they were already gone.

Chapter 8

Saturday morning, Maggie got the call that Sally had suffered a stroke. She was in the hospital, and not doing well. Sally's niece knew that Maggie and she were close, so she thought maybe Maggie would want to come visit.

Maggie called the church to invite Harmony to come along. The church phone rang and went to voicemail. That was unusual. Maggie tried again. Same thing. She didn't usually work in the office on Saturdays. Tiny usually covered for her, and called her or Pete if something came up that he couldn't handle.

Maggie tried Harmony's cell phone, but that didn't work either. Harmony must be out of minutes. She usually was. So she drove to the church.

She waved to the people hanging out in the unofficial smoking area and then went inside to hunt Harmony down and immediately noticed there was no one in the office. She tried the door. It was locked. This was not good. If someone came in looking for a place to stay, there would be no one there to help them. She was wondering how she was going to find Tiny without going into the men's part of the shelter, which was off-limits to females. Then she rounded a corner and almost ran into Pete.

"Hey there! We really should put up mirrors to prevent collisions like this," Pete joked.

"Yeah, I know. Where is everyone?"

"I dunno. Who you lookin' for?"

"Well, I'm looking for Harmony, but why isn't Tiny in the office?"

"Pastor Chris kicked him out."

"What?"

"Yeah, he didn't really say why, but I think he didn't want Tiny checking people in."

"Why on earth not?"

"I don't know, but you know, Tiny's not the sharpest tool in the shed. Maybe he wanted someone more professional in there."

"Like who?"

"I dunno, you?"

Maggie looked exasperated. "I can't be here round-the-clock."

"I know. That's why we need to clone you."

"Look, Pete, for now, can you cover the office? I'll let you in. You can play Panda Pop or something. Just in case someone shows up and needs to be checked in? You can call me if you run into any trouble."

"Sure. I'll do it just for the chance of calling you."

"Thank you, Pete. You're a lifesaver." She turned and headed back toward the office.

"That's what all the ladies say."

She laughed. "Don't make me laugh. I don't want to encourage you."

Pete put up both his hands. "Hey, I can't help it if I'm charming and witty."

Maggie unlocked the door for him. "Right," she said and headed away.

"The last time I saw Harmony, she was getting a game of Sorry out of the library," Pete called after her.

"OK, thanks," Maggie called back. Sure enough, Maggie found Harmony in her room playing Sorry with Daniel, Jessica, and Jayden. Well, Jayden was sort of playing. He was mostly just chewing on the ice ring. "Hey," Maggie said, and walked through the open door. "I just got some bad news. Sally has had a stroke, and I'm going to go see her in the hospital."

"Well, what is she, like a hundred and ten?" Jessica asked.

"No," Maggie said, "but she is well into her eighties, I think. So, do you want to come with me?" Maggie asked Harmony.

"Definitely," Harmony said to Maggie, and then to Jessica, "Can you watch Daniel?"

"I want to come," Daniel said.

Harmony looked at Maggie.

"Fine with me, kiddo, but I don't think it's going to be much fun," Maggie said.

"I know," Daniel said.

"OK then, get your shoes on," Harmony said. "And have you brushed your teeth yet today?" Daniel shook his head. "OK, then do that too."

Harmony stood up and started looking for her own shoes as Daniel left the room with a toothbrush.

"Um, he knows he can't heal Sally, right?" Maggie asked.

"Not sure," Harmony said. "Maybe he can."

Sally was in a coma. When Maggie, Harmony, and Daniel entered her room, they found a younger woman sitting beside her bed, holding her hand.

"Hi," Maggie said softly. "You must be Sally's niece? I'm Maggie. We spoke on the phone?"

"Of course," the young woman said, standing. "I'm Emily. Thanks so much for coming. Sally spoke very highly of you. She just loved to go to your little church salon."

Maggie smiled and nodded. "This is mine and Sally's friend Harmony, and her son Daniel."

"It's a pleasure—" Emily started, but Daniel silenced her when he ran the four steps it took to get to her and then wrapped his little arms around her waist. "Oh my!" Emily said.

"I'm so sorry," Harmony said, reaching to pull Daniel back.

"No, it's quite all right. I like hugs," she said with a small laugh. She rubbed Daniel's small back as if she was the one comforting him.

Eventually, he took a step back. Daniel looked Emily in the eye and said, "She's going to die."

"Daniel!" Harmony snapped.

But Emily held a hand up to her, effectively stalling the reprimand. "It's OK. The boy is just telling the truth."

"But she is ready," Daniel added.

Emily smiled through tears. "Yes, I know."

That night, there was a lot of commotion in the men's area of the shelter.

Dwight had come back from the bar tanked and cantankerous. At first, the men just thought it funny and laughed as Dwight staggered around crashing into bunks, kicking coolers, and knocking over trash cans.

But then Chief looked at Dwight the wrong way and awoke the primal alpha within him. Dwight sauntered up to Chief until he was chest to chest with him. Chief took a step back, instinctively, but then appeared to think better of it and stood his ground.

"You got something to say?" Dwight growled.

"Yeah, I do," Chief said firmly. "There's no drinking here."

Dwight's mouth spread in an exaggerated, but joyless, smile. He took a step back from Chief and spread his arms. "Do you see any drinking?" He looked from one side of the room to the other, as more than a dozen men looked on, and asked again, "Do you? Do you? I don't see anyone drinking." He stepped forward and slapped Chief on the chest, too hard to be playful. "You don't need to worry there, Champ. There's no drinking here." He stepped back again. "Isn't that right, guys? We wouldn't drink in church, now would we?"

Chief stomped out of the room. Two men, Randy and Fred, followed him. But where Chief veered off toward the kitchen, Randy and Fred headed for the door. They went through it, out into the dark, and silently but quickly walked to the convenience store, which was only a quarter of a mile away.

Within twenty minutes, they had returned to the crowded sleeping quarters with three half-gallons of Black Velvet.

"What are you, made of money?" Pete asked Randy.

"Nope, just sold my food stamps." Randy laughed.

"What? To who?"

"Amber."

"Who's Amber?"

Randy rolled his eyes. "You know. Amber. She comes here like every few weeks and buys food stamps. A whole bunch of us sell to her." Randy paused and looked around the room. A few others nodded.

Looking disgusted, Pete left the room.

No one else did. Everyone else stayed in the room to partake. And partake they did.

When Pete returned to the room to go to bed, most of them were still up, hooting and hollering. Several of them were already passed out, and the room smelled of vomit. Pete lay down, pulled the covers over his head, and tried to fall asleep. Eventually he did.

When he woke up, he groped around for his glasses. They weren't there. He sat up and looked around. No glasses. It's hard to see a missing object when the missing object is what allows you to see, and eventually Pete gave up.

He tried to wake the others up, to ask them if anyone had seen his glasses. None of them would wake up. None of them would even acknowledge his question. Then he heard Chief from across the room, "They probably took 'em. Did something with 'em."

"Why would someone steal my glasses?"

"Why wouldn't they?" Chief asked sardonically, and left the room.

The men slept through breakfast, and then they slept through Sunday morning service. But it wasn't easy to notice their absence, as the room was full of new people, several of whom were holding white canes.

Squinting, Pete scanned the sanctuary for any clues as to the whereabouts of his glasses, and then gave up and headed for the pastor's office. "Pastor?"

Chris was seated at his desk. He didn't look up. "Yes?"

"Someone took my glasses, and I can't hardly see without them."

Chris looked up at him. "Well, I'm not sure what you want me to do about it?"

In his past, Pete had been accused of having a hair-trigger temper. In a flash, he proved that allegation true. Pete slammed the door to Chris's office so hard the whole wall shook. Then he put both hands on Chris's desk, and leaned forward menacingly. Chris recoiled in his chair.

"Well, you know, you're the *pastor*, and it's sort of your job to figure this type of ..." He paused to avoid cursing. "This type of *stuff* out. Who else am I supposed to ask? Just go in there and tell them to give my glasses back! It's your *job*!"

Chris stood up, and began to walk around his desk, still giving Pete a wide berth. "My job is to shepherd God's sheep." He opened the door. "My job is to preach, not to police. I'm sorry that you think someone took your glasses. But I cannot help you." He stood beside the door as if waiting for Pete to exit through it.

Pete had other ideas. In two quick strides, he was nose to nose with the pastor, and the fear was apparent in the pastor's pale face. Pete drew his right arm back. Chris closed his eyes and appeared to brace himself as Pete's fist hit the wall just beside Chris's head. The drywall crumbled beneath the force, leaving a giant hole in the wall just to the left of Chris's framed divinity degree.

Pete had stormed out of the office before Chris even opened his eyes. Once he did, he looked around to be sure he was alone. Then he shut and locked his office door. He took several long breaths and then he dialed 911.

Chris stayed in his office until the police arrived. Then he came out so he could point to the offender. The worship team, which was now composed of a rotation of volunteer musicians from other churches, people whom Chris and the elders had recruited to replace the regulars, had already started playing, and Pete was in the front row, with his deficient eyes closed, his mouth open, and his hands up in the air in praise.

One of the police officers asked him to step out into the aisle. Pete did not look surprised. The worship team stopped playing. The other police officer asked Pete to put his hands behind his back. He did so with what looked like stoic pride. As the officer snapped the cuffs onto his wrists, he quietly said, "You are under arrest ..." and led him down the middle of the sanctuary and out through the doors. Pete never said a word.

It was only then that Chris came into the sanctuary and took a seat near the front. The worship team picked up where they'd left off, and some of the people sang along. After a few songs, they left the stage, and Chris took their place. "Welcome!" he said, with arms spread wide. "We're so glad to have you here to worship with us at Open Door."

Chris's message that morning was on integrity. He offered several Scriptures and a few present-day anecdotes, and then closed in prayer. And the congregation waited patiently as he did so. When he finished his prayer, the worship team had reclaimed their positions up front. It was clear that Chris was done and was headed for his seat, and someone called out from the back row, "Will there be a healing today?"

Chris looked in the general direction of the speaker, but didn't seem sure of exactly who had spoken up. "Sure," he said with a forced smile. "I would be happy to pray for anyone who would like to come forward."

"Not you," the voice called. "We want the boy."

"Yes," another voice joined in. "We came to see Daniel."

Chris could see the second speaker and so looked him in the eye. "I'm sorry, what?"

The speaker, a middle-aged man wearing a pressed suit, stepped out into the aisle. "No disrespect, Pastor, but we've come to see

Daniel, the boy who heals. He laid hands on someone last week, and the next morning, he could see."

Chris appeared to be speechless.

Daniel made his way to the front.

When Chris saw him, his head snapped toward the child. "Sit down," he barked.

Daniel stopped walking. "No," he said calmly.

"Sit down," Chris hollered.

Daniel stood firm.

"Now hold on a minute," Chief said, and started belligerently toward to the front. But an elder's hand on his shoulder stopped him.

"Thank you, sir. I'll handle this," Phil said condescendingly. "You can return to your seat."

Chief didn't return to his seat, but he did stop his march forward. He folded his arms across his chest and stood still.

Phil reached Chris and whispered something lengthy into his ear while the entire congregation waited silently. Not even a baby whimpered. Finally, Chris offered a broad smile. "My apologies, everyone. This has all caught me off guard, and I don't always respond well to surprises. Of course, if God wants to do something here, who am I to stop him?" He chuckled and then motioned for Daniel to take his spot in front.

Daniel did. No one moved. No one seemed to know what to do next. Finally Harmony spoke up, "Why don't you line up in front of Daniel, anyone who wants prayer."

And the people came forward. And they stood in front of the eight-year-old boy. And one by one they spoke to Daniel. And Daniel took each person's hand into his own as he quietly prayed for each illness, injury, and disability. It took nearly an hour. Most of the church guests left before they were officially dismissed. The elders left as well. But Chief stayed. Chief waited till the last prayer had been prayed. Then he watched Daniel, exhausted, collapse into his mother's arms. And he watched Chris walk toward the sound booth. And he followed. And he heard Chris say, "Of course, we won't be airing this episode." And he heard the man with the camera say, "We'll have to talk to our producer. Not sure what he'll want to do with it. We'll let you know." And he heard Chris retort, "Don't bother. I'll go call him right now." And Chief followed Chris to, and into, his office before Chris could even shut the door.

"What?" Chris snapped.

"Did you know that half the men were missing this morning?"

Chris sat down. He looked at the haggard man before him. "What?" he asked again. It appeared that he genuinely did not understand.

Chief licked his lips. "Randy and Fred brought a bunch of booze back to the shelter last night and a bunch of guys got lit. They're still sleeping it off right now. A whole mess of 'em, including your hero Dwight."

At the mention of Dwight's name, Chris's expression went from mild interest to complete dismissal. "OK, thank you. I'll take care of it," he said, looking down at his desk.

When Galen answered the phone, a robot told him he had a collect call from Somerset County Jail. Galen groaned. This was not the first time.

"Will you accept the charges?" the robot asked.

"Yes."

"Hey, G. Sorry 'bout this. Can you come bail me out?"

Galen recognized Pete's voice. "Bail you out for what?"

"You weren't in church?" Pete sounded shocked.

"No, sorry, we decided that six days in a row was enough. We thought we'd rest on the seventh day."

"OK, OK, sorry. Don't need to get snippy. Look I kinda lost it on Chris. I put my fist through his wall. I wasn't gonna hit him, promise. But apparently he's a wuss in addition to an arrogant hypocrite. Can you please come bail me out? I promise I'm good for it. I just really don't have anyone else to call."

"Good grief, Pete. I don't have that kind of cash!"

"I know, I know, I'm sorry. Do you know if Maggie still has access to the slush fund? I think Pastor Dan would've bailed me out."

"Pastor Dan wouldn't have had to bail you out. They would've just released you to him. Come to think of it, you wouldn't be in this mess because you wouldn't have put a hole in his wall. What did he do to get you so riled up?"

"Someone stole my glasses."

"And you think the pastor did it?"

"No, of course not. But I told him, and he just didn't care. I was so mad, because I couldn't see."

"All right. Um, sit tight. We'll try to figure something out. But seriously, get comfortable, 'cause we are poor as crows."

"OK, G. Thanks a million. Thank Maggie for me too. You guys are the best. Don't know what that place would do without you. Sure do wish you'd been there today."

Chapter 9

Just before Monday night Bible study, Chief approached Galen.

"We've got a problem," he said brusquely.

"We?" Galen asked.

"Yes, we. A whole bunch of people got drunk here Saturday."

Galen rubbed his head and sighed. "Yeah," he said, thoughtfully, "I guess I'm kind of surprised that hasn't happened before now."

"Well, it has, occasionally, but Pastor Dan always dealt with it. Most people didn't mess with it, because they didn't want to disappoint the guy, and they didn't want to get kicked out. But these guys, it was like they didn't even care. It was like they knew that nothing was gonna happen to 'em for it. And I guess they were right. 'Cause nothing has happened to them. Especially that Dwight guy. There is something seriously wrong with that jarhead. He's just such a …"

"Bully?" Galen offered. "Does he drive you nuts because he's a bigger bully than you are?"

"I ain't no bully!" Chief said, aghast. "And thanks for nothing, G." He turned, swearing at Galen as he walked away.

Galen dragged his feet toward the front of the room and then looked at the stage, obviously confused. "Where is everyone?" he asked no one in particular.

A young woman named Annie answered him. "We don't have a worship team anymore."

"What?" Galen asked her. "Why?"

"Pastor Chris couldn't find anyone to volunteer—"

Galen interrupted her, "What? We used to have people fighting over it."

"I know, but the homeless can't do it anymore, and he couldn't find any volunteers to play on weeknights. He said we'd just have music on the weekends. You know, when the cameras are rolling."

Galen gave her a long look. "Not much gets by you, huh, Annie?"

She shook her head. "I wish that more did."

"I know what you mean," he said, and took his place up front. "Welcome, everyone. Let's open with a word of prayer."

After Galen said "amen," he lifted his head, opened his eyes, and found himself looking into young Daniel's eyes. "You know what?" he began. "I was going to talk about some verses from Mark tonight, but instead, let's talk about miracles."

Someone made a scoffing sound, and Galen looked at the spot where Dwight usually sat, but Dwight had moved to the back row.

"We've been having a lot of miracles around here lately. Actually, we've been having miracles for years, but these newest ones do seem to be more obvious. I think it's important that we recognize these healings for what they are. Let's look at Isaiah 55. Randy, would you please read verses 8 and 9?"

Randy pulled a pew Bible out from under his seat and stood. He put on his reading glasses and then flipped through most of the Old Testament as he searched for Isaiah. Finally, he cleared his throat and carefully read the verses, "'For my thoughts are not your thoughts, nor are your ways my ways,' declares the Lord. 'For as the heavens are higher than the earth, so are my ways higher than your ways and my thoughts than your thoughts.'"

"Thank you, Randy," Galen said. "So, God's ways are higher than our ways. So, obviously, we're not always going to understand what he is up to. But we can take comfort in the fact that he *is* working. He *is* still here. He *does* still care. Pastor Dan left us, but God has not. He is showing us his power through this young boy, Daniel. We don't know why. Maybe it's because Daniel has great faith. Matthew 18 tells us we should all have faith like a child, right? But it's not really about Daniel." Galen paused and looked at his young friend. Daniel was smiling. "And it's not really about any of us either. We are put on this earth to glorify God. God is doing something here, and we don't understand it, but we don't have to."

A man in the back row stood up. "I know what God's up to."

"OK," Galen said. "And you are?"

"I am a prophet of the Lord."

"No he isn't!" Daniel said in a small voice. Harmony shushed him.

"OK, great. And what is your name?"

"I am Abdiel."

A man in front of him snickered. "His name is Dave," he said, and several people laughed.

"OK, Abdiel," Galen said. "We are glad you are here. Now if I can continue—"

"You can't continue," Dave said. "Because you are a liar! You are not a prophet of God!" The man began to walk toward Galen. Galen calmly set his Bible down and squared his body toward his advance. Maggie pulled out her cell phone. "I," the man bellowed, "am a prophet of God. God has revealed his will to me, and has sent me to tell you that there are angels here. There are angels in this room right now." Dave reached Galen but then turned to face his audience. He held one fist up in the air. "But these angels are angry! They have come to pour out God's wrath on us! We will suffer! We will burn!"

"Dave, please," Galen tried. "Thank you for your prophecy, but can you please have a seat?"

Dave didn't seem to hear him. "We will burn for eternity! We will suffer at God's hand, because we are all evil!"

Young Daniel tried to stand up, but Harmony pulled him back down to his seat, wrapped her arms around him and put her hand over his mouth.

"We are an abomination, and God is going to wipe us from the face of the planet!"

Maggie discreetly wagged her phone at Galen, letting him know that help was on the way. But apparently Iraq Veteran Dwight Schultz didn't want to wait. In six quick strides he was in front of Dave and before anyone knew what was happening, Dwight's right fist was connecting with the left side of Dave's jaw, making a sickening cracking sound. Helplessly, Galen tried to catch Dave as he crumpled to the floor, but it happened too fast. And then, as everyone else appeared frozen in shock, Dwight straddled Dave's limp body and knelt. And then Dwight hit him in the face. And then he hit him again. Finally, Galen seemed to spring to life and he tried to pull Dwight off the beaten man. Immediately, Dwight turned toward Galen and, though he was off balance, took a swing at Galen's head. It connected, but only weakly. Several other men joined the fray then, and after a few painful minutes of wrestling, kicking, and flailing, four of the men had Dwight Schultz pinned to the carpet.

As they held him there, the man seemed to run out of steam. After a few minutes, Dwight said, "I'm good! Let go! You can let me up. I'm good! Let go of me!"

The other men looked at Galen for leadership, and Galen acquiesced, though it wasn't clear whether he thought letting Dwight up was a good idea, or whether he was just exhausted.

Dwight stood up, brushed off his jeans, and then rubbed his jaw as he calmly walked out of the sanctuary.

Galen and the other men just sat where they were, on the floor, quietly, waiting for the police to arrive.

The next morning, as Chief stepped into the shower stall, he almost stepped on a hypodermic needle.

It took him a second to realize what it was, but as soon as he did, he stooped to pick it up. And then he grabbed a small towel, which he held in front of his waist with his left hand as he walked out into the hallway. And then down the corridor he went, bare-butted, with his towel in his left hand and the needle held out in front of him in his right. Down the corridor he went, in front of men, women, children, and God, all the way to the office.

"Chief!" Maggie exclaimed in horror. "What are you doing?!"

Oblivious to her real question, he wiggled the needle in front of her. "I just found this! In the shower!"

"What is it?" Maggie scrunched up her nose.

"It's a needle," Chief said, as if he was talking to the stupidest person alive.

"I know it's a needle, but why was there a needle in the shower?"

"It's a heroin needle! I don't know why it was in the shower! But that's not OK! I almost stepped on it! I could've gotten AIDS and died! Where is our fearless pastor?"

Maggie sighed. "No idea. Look, just leave that ... thing ... on the windowsill. I'll tell him about it when he comes in, *if* he comes in. You go get dressed!"

Grudgingly, Chief turned to go, and Maggie averted her eyes back to the pile of mail in front of her. There was far more mail than usual. There were letters *to* Daniel and letters to the church *about* Daniel. Everybody wanted to meet Daniel. As she sat reading, Tiny walked into the office.

"Hey, Tiny! What's up?"

"What's all that?" he asked, pointing his chin at the handwritten letters.

"Letters about Daniel."

She placed another one on a neat pile.

"That pile for Pastor?" Tiny asked.

"Yep."

"Why not his mum?"

Maggie looked at him for a second. "You're right." She stuffed the letters into her purse. "I'll show them to Harmony later. But these," she said, pointing to some checks, "these I can't really hide." The church had just received three checks bearing names she didn't recognize. One was for twenty dollars, one for one hundred, and one for one thousand. The thousand dollar check read, "For the ministry of Daniel" in the memo line. It had come with a note from the woman who had lung cancer, the woman who was now cancer-free.

When Chief finally got showered and dressed, he made his way to the kitchen for another cup of coffee. And he ran smack into Dwight.

"What are you doing here?" Chief barked.

"I live here."

"Yeah, but you got taken out of here in cuffs last night."

"Yep. And now I'm back." Dwight took a bite out of a stale donut. Then with his mouth full, he said, "Crazy, right?"

"Who bailed you out?"

"No one," Dwight said, his mouth still full. "I was never charged. Chris came and smoothed things over. He said he'd keep an eye on me."

Chief stared at Dwight speechlessly as Dwight sauntered out of the kitchen.

Chief prepared his coffee and then carried it up the stairs and down the hallway to the office. Annie was leaning against the doorframe, talking to Maggie about a spoon shortage. Chief pushed her out of the way.

"Hey!" Annie shouted.

"Chief!" Maggie exclaimed. She stood up and put her hands on her hips. "You can't treat people like that!"

"Oh yeah? Says who?"

"Me!" Tiny said, rising from his seat in the corner.

"So that jarhead jerk can beat the living snot out of Dave, and nothing happens to him, but I bump into Annie and suddenly I'm the bad guy? What is this place coming to?"

"Maybe you've just been here too long," Annie offered in a small voice from behind him.

Chief wheeled around. "Oh yeah, you're one to talk. You ever worked a day in your life?"

Annie skulked off down the hall.

"I'll find some spoons, Annie!" Maggie called after her. Then she looked at Chief, "You don't need to act like that, you know?"

"Did you hear what I just said? Dwight is back. He tried to kill someone last night and now he's walking around like he owns the place!"

Maggie returned her attention to her computer. "I don't know what to tell you, Chief. I just work here."

"Have you shown him the needle yet?"

"Nope. He hasn't been in."

"How long *have* you lived here, anyway?" Tiny asked.

"Dunno," Chief said and stomped away.

Tiny looked at Maggie. "Not sure," she said. "My guess would be five years?"

"Five years?" Tiny looked horrified. "I can't imagine living here for five years. This place is awful."

Maggie looked as if she might cry as she started searching for used spoons for sale.

Pastor Chris did show up, shortly after lunch. As soon as he was through the door, Maggie handed him a stack of paperwork, including orders that needed to be approved by the treasurer and the checks that had come in for Daniel.

Chris didn't even look at her. He just took the paperwork and mumbled a thanks.

"Also, Sally Ladd passed away. We need to schedule her funeral."

"Who's Sally Ladd?"

Maggie took a deep breath. "She's an older member of the church. Has been coming here for years. She had a stroke last week. Her family has since decided to let her go."

"Ah, I see. Well, that's too bad. Go ahead and schedule the funeral, if her family wants it done here."

"When will you be available to do it?"

Chris turned to go into the office as he said, "Just schedule it. If I'm not available, we'll find someone to fill in for me."

Maggie followed him as far as the doorway to his office. "And there's one more thing."

Chris looked up.

Maggie plucked the needle from its perch on the windowsill beside where she stood. "This was found in the men's showers this morning."

Chris sighed. "OK, thanks for letting me know. You can throw it away."

"Don't we have to dispose of it properly or something? Isn't it hazardous?"

Chris rolled his eyes. "Give it to me," he said, and held out the stack of papers. She put the needle on top of the papers, and then stood still as Chris went into his office and shut the door.

That Wednesday, when Galen showed up to lead Bible study, Chris said to him, "I'm sorry, I forgot to call you. You won't be needed tonight."

"What? Why?" Galen asked.

"I'm going to take over Wednesday nights. You're welcome to stay and worship of course, but we won't need you to lead."

"Oh," Galen said. And Chris walked away.

Galen peeked into the sanctuary, where a full worship band was preparing to start, and a film crew was rolling.

Chapter 10

Maggie scheduled Sally's memorial service for Thursday afternoon. More than a hundred people came to celebrate Sally's full life. Though the people sleeping at the church were not obligated to come, they were welcome to, and many of them did. Sally had always been sweet and kind to her church body, and their affection for her was apparent at the service.

It turned out that Chris was available to officiate Sally's service, and Sally's niece was grateful that a professional pastor would be in charge. At least, she started out that way. Then he made his way to the front, spread his arms in a welcoming gesture, and said, "Welcome friends and family of *Shirley* Ladd."

Several people immediately looked down at their copy of the program Maggie had printed up. Then they looked back at the pastor, their eyes full of disappointment and disgust.

On Thursday night, several of the men went out together. They walked to the nearest bar. Dwight had some money, and the more rounds he bought, the more willing he was to buy more rounds.

At 1:30 a.m., Chief woke to a pounding on the window. He rolled over to look and before he saw anything at all, he heard their drunken laughter.

"Idiots," he mumbled as he rolled over.

The banging got louder.

Chief lay still.

Another man, Kevin, got up and walked toward the window.

"Don't let them in," Chief growled.

"They're not going to stop, and I want to go to sleep eventually," Kevin said. "It's really the only part of life I enjoy." He unlocked the window and opened it.

The men tumbled through it, reeking of booze and marijuana. "The door was locked," Randy said and then laughed uproariously. Most of the others followed suit.

"That's 'cause it's after curfew, you imbecile," Duke said, and they all laughed even harder.

"Shut up!" Chief barked.

"Make me, old man," Dwight said, sounding far closer to sober than he could've been, given how much alcohol he had just consumed.

The next morning Pastor Chris asked everyone to come to the sanctuary. It took some effort, but the men who were up managed to get the others out of bed to join them. And so they staggered, eyes half-closed, into the sanctuary and fell into the pews.

"I don't think it's *ever* smelled this bad in here," Maggie said to Harmony. "And that's really saying something."

"They're drunk," Daniel said matter-of-factly.

"I'm guessing that's what the meeting is about," Maggie said, more to Daniel than to Harmony.

Maggie was wrong.

"I've called you all here today because we have a situation. Apparently, some of you have been smoking outside, on the other side of the parking lot. I've taken the liberty of cleaning your little smoking area up, and I would ask you to refrain from smoking on the property. A potential donor has contacted me and expressed concern that they are giving money to people who can afford cigarettes. Now I know"—Chris held up his hands in a completely unbelievable gesture of empathy—"it is hard to quit smoking, and I'm not asking you to. I'm just asking you not to smoke on the property."

Chief stood up. "Are you crazy?"

"That's enough out of you," Chris tried.

"No really, are you crazy? We've got people shooting up in the bathroom and drunks climbing through windows, and you're worried about the smoking area?" Chief turned and stormed out of the sanctuary, mumbling obscenities as he left.

As Maggie opened the mail that day, she saw a check from JCTV, and it was much bigger than she'd ever have expected. Chris walked by her as she was staring at it, and ripped it out of her hands. "I'll take that," he said abruptly. "There's absolutely no reason for you to be opening my private mail."

"I'm sorry," Maggie said, sounding quite sincere. "It had the church address on it."

"Yes, but it was to *my name*," he said, shoving the envelope in her face. "Can you read?"

Maggie's eyes grew wide and filled with tears.

She slowly stood. "I'll do you one better," she said quietly, her voice choked with the oncoming flood. "I'll let you do all the mail from now on." She scooped it up and dropped it all into his arms, which were not ready for the onslaught, so most of the mail fell to the floor.

Maggie picked up her purse and said to Tiny, "I'm leaving for a while, Tiny. Thank you for all of your help." And she left through the front door of Open Door Church.

On Sunday, Daniel met the Turney family at the door.

"Where have you been?" he demanded.

Galen laughed. He was being scolded by an eight-year-old. "What are you talking about, little man? I was just here on Friday. Where's your mom?"

Daniel put his hands on his hips. "Maggie never came to church on Friday. She wasn't here yesterday either. Where have you been?" he asked, looking up at Maggie.

"Come on, let's go play," Elijah said, pulling on Daniel's hand.

"I can't," Daniel said, still looking up at Maggie.

Maggie sighed. "It's complicated, honey. I don't think I'm going to be able to help in the office anymore."

"You can't do that," Daniel said.

"OK," Maggie said, and gently turned his shoulders toward the sanctuary. "Let's go talk to your mom."

Harmony wasn't even in the sanctuary yet, but Daniel walked on ahead of the Turneys. He walked clear to the stage and then fell to his knees. He folded his hands in prayer and bowed his head.

"I maintain," Galen said quietly as he sat down, "that is one strange kid."

Maggie giggled. "Oh stop it. He's precious. I wish I had faith like his."

Daniel stayed in that position until the worship team took the stage. Then he made his way to the row in front of the Turneys, just as Harmony was coming down the aisle. As the worship team started to play, Daniel looked at Maggie. "I just prayed for you."

"Why, thank you," Maggie said.

"I prayed that God would stop you from leaving." Daniel looked at Galen and then back at Maggie. "You can't leave. We need you." Then Daniel turned toward the front and began to sing in his clear, confident, high-pitched voice, with both his small hands in the air.

Daniel and the Turneys were so focused on their interpersonal drama that they didn't seem to notice at first how many new faces were in the congregation that morning. There were several. Pastor Chris welcomed them with pomp aplenty. He made several announcements, which seemed to be geared more toward the viewers at home than at the people in the sanctuary, telling them when they could view the services on television and online. He even announced a podcast, which brought a stunned look to Maggie's face. "What will he think of next?" she asked Galen.

"And I'm pleased to announce that I've been invited to speak at this year's New England Pastors' Convention in Springfield, Massachusetts," Chris declared. "It seems that other churches in New England and even beyond are interested in doing what we're doing here. And they want me to come train them as to how to get such a project going."

Galen frowned.

"Elder Phil will be filling in for me here while I'm gone."

Galen frowned harder.

"And I will also be taking a few of my success stories with me." Chris paused to smile at Dwight. "So they can share their testimonies, about how this church has saved them."

Tiny raised his hand.

Chris ignored him.

Tiny waved his hand in the air. Tiny was not an easy man to ignore.

"We'll take prayer requests tomorrow," Chris said to Tiny without looking at him, and moved to pick up his Bible, signifying he was about to get serious about preaching.

"I don't have no prayer request," Tiny declared, his hand still up in the air.

Chris looked down at his Bible. "If you would all turn with me to Joshua chapter 1."

"Hey!" Tiny shouted. "I was just going to say that you should take the boy. You should take Daniel. He's a real success story. Born and raised in this church, he's a miracle worker!"

Chris's cheeks flushed. "Thank you, Tiny."

But others weren't so quick to dismiss Tiny's idea. Duke, from the back row, said, "You really should take him, Pastor. People would love it."

Joyce from the right side offered, "He could heal people while he was there," while Liam from the left said, "I want to go too! I'm a success story!" Many of the guests laughed at this, as Liam was far from a success story.

Chris gave a panicked glance at the camera. It seemed he had lost control of the service.

A young woman near the back stood up timidly and put her hand in the air. Chris didn't seem to see it. "Excuse me," she spoke meekly. The people seated near her gave her their attention, but the rest of the place was still chuckling about Liam. "Excuse me," she said more loudly. The laughter died down as the rest of the congregation gave her their attention. "I'm sorry, I don't mean to interrupt, but since we're on the subject. Is the little boy here? I've brought my father here." The congregation looked down at her side to find an older gentleman sitting partially doubled over as if afflicted with a terrible stomach ache. "We've traveled a long way, because he's seen many doctors, but he's in terrible pain, and the doctors can't quite figure out what's wrong with him ..."

Everyone was so focused on the young woman and her father that no one seemed to notice that Daniel was already moving up the side of the sanctuary toward them, until he entered their row. "Are you him?" the young woman asked.

Daniel nodded.

"I'm Lily," the woman said, and she smiled. She sat back down beside her father. Daniel sat down on the other side of him.

"Hi," Daniel said to the man. "I'm Daniel."

"Hello, young fella. My name is Walter. I've been having this awful stomach pain for several months now. Can't seem to eat anything—"

Daniel placed an uninvited, but seemingly welcome, hand on the man's stomach, effectively halting his explanation. Daniel closed his eyes and then just sat there, silently, with his hand on Walter's abdomen. Every eye in the place was on Daniel. The pastor's eyes slid to the camera. The camera was also on Daniel.

A few minutes later, Daniel opened his eyes. He smiled at Walter and said, "I hope you feel better soon."

"Thank you, son," Walter said.

"Me!" Someone cried out from the other side of the room. "Me! I'm next!"

Daniel looked confused, but he headed toward her.

"Actually, if I could just have your attention," Chris tried, but no one paid him any mind. The camera followed the boy across the room.

Daniel stopped in front of the woman who had cried out. "What's wrong?"

"I have MS," the woman said.

"I don't know if God will heal you, but I will ask him to."

"OK," the woman said.

Daniel knelt in front of her, put his hands on her knees, and prayed silently, his brow furrowed.

When he had finished, he stood up, turned toward the pastor and nodded to him, as if to suggest that the pastor could continue. Chris's annoyance was all over his face. He cleared his throat, and grudgingly, people turned their attention back to the preacher as the child made his way back to his seat beside his mother.

As soon as he sat, Maggie leaned forward and whispered, "I won't leave you, Daniel."

Chapter 11

After church, the guests gathered in the undercroft for lunch. Daniel was nowhere to be seen, so people weren't shy about talking about him, not that they necessarily would've been had he been there.

"How is he doing it?" Annie asked Fred.

"Dunno," Fred answered, his mouth full of pudding.

"I don't think he is doing it. I think it's God," Joyce said.

"Yeah, well, someone should figure out how to make some money off the kid. None of us would be homeless anymore," Annie said.

"How would *you* make money off him? Harmony maybe. But you?"

Harmony heard her name, and her head snapped around. "What are you saying?"

"Nothing," Fred answered.

"No. What? Tell me!" she demanded. Their silence and shameful looks answered her question. "Good grief, you creeps. Leave him alone. He's just a kid." She turned her back to them.

"He's a freak," someone muttered under his breath.

She wheeled back around to face the gossipers. "You're just jealous," she spat. "You're jealous of his faith. The kid believes, OK? He believes God can do this stuff, so God does. It's that simple." She slammed her tray down on the table beside them, her food untouched, and stomped out of the room and up the stairs.

After a few seconds of stunned silence, Annie asked, "Think I could take her pudding cup?"

On Wednesday night, Galen, Maggie, and the kids were at home, enjoying a peaceful supper. Galen and Maggie had decided that, since Chris had taken over Wednesday Bible studies, Wednesdays would be reserved for family time. Galen had already promised a game of rummy after the dishes were done.

As Galen was helping himself to another scoop of mashed potatoes, his cell rang. Maggie gave him a dirty look, but he answered it anyway. He listened to the caller for about five seconds and then stood up and turned on the television.

Maggie followed.

Galen turned to Channel 5, and the local news appeared on the screen. And there was Melanie, looking even more disheveled than usual, with a microphone in front of her. "Fraud? No, cuss not. The kid ain't no fraud. Nobody could fake that."

A pretty reporter retrieved the microphone. "Thank you," she said to Melanie, and then to the camera, "This is Lindsey Michaels reporting live from Open Door Church in Mattawooptock."

"What on earth was that?" Maggie asked.

Galen still had the phone up to his ear. "What came before that?" he asked. He listened, looking sickly as he did, and then he nodded. "OK, then. Thanks for calling … yep. Bye."

Maggie's eyes were wide. "Well?"

"Apparently, that woman, the one who had MS? Well, she isn't healed. So she's telling the world that Daniel's a fraud."

"What's going to happen to Daniel, Daddy?" Isaiah asked, with the same wide eyes as his mother.

"Nothing, honey. Absolutely nothing is going to happen to Daniel. I'll make sure of it. Daniel just tries to help people. And sometimes, well, people aren't always grateful."

"But Daniel said to her, 'Hey, this might not work,'" Maggie said defensively.

"I know, I know," Galen said, taking Maggie in his arms. He kissed the top of her head. "This is no big deal, really, just annoying."

"Oh, I'm annoyed all right," Maggie mumbled into his shoulder. "The kid heals the multitudes, and the news could care less, but let one woman complain, and they're all over it."

Galen chuckled. "Yep," he said, and let go of his wife. "So I say the best thing we can do right now is to finish our supper."

Friday afternoon, Pete strolled back into church and into the office as if nothing had happened.

"Can I check in again, ma'am?" he asked Maggie.

Maggie looked up, smiled at her friend, and then got up to give him a hug. "Welcome home, Pete! We've missed you."

"How'd you get out?" Tiny asked, without getting up.

"Nice to see you too," Pete said to Tiny. Then he gave Maggie a smile, and she returned it, as if they shared a secret. "Well, Tiny, an anonymous friend posted my bail."

"Well, good," Maggie said quickly, and returned to her seat. "Glad to have you back. Did you ever find your glasses?"

"Sure didn't. Can't see a thing. So, what have I missed around here?"

Maggie rolled her eyes. "Good grief, a *lot.*"

Tiny took a deep breath. "The kid keeps healing people, everybody keeps getting drunk, Randy has a whole bunch of weed under his mattress, Annie and Fred hooked up, Ellyn got an apartment, and our new pastor hates homeless people."

Pete laughed. "Well then, I guess I'm just about caught up. Thanks, Tiny. So whose new truck is in the parking lot?"

Maggie raised an eyebrow. "No idea. I haven't seen any new faces today."

"No," Pete said. "Not a truck that's new to our parking lot. I mean a *brand spankin'* new truck. I'm not that blind. Still has ten-day plates. Must've cost forty grand."

Maggie shook her head. "I can't imagine," she said dismissively.

"Well, it says 'Open Door Homeless Shelter' on the side of it. Does that give you any clue?" Pete asked.

"What?! Isn't that a little ironic? A new truck with homeless painted on the side? Are you sure?"

Pete looked annoyed. "Yes, I walked right up to it so I could read it!"

Just then, Elder Phil walked in. Another man they didn't know trailed behind him. "Did you get a new truck?" Tiny asked Phil.

Maggie stifled a giggle.

"No," Phil said, obviously irked. "That's Pastor Chris's truck. We had to get him something reliable to take to Massachusetts." Phil turned his attention to Maggie. "Maggie, this gentleman will be installing an air conditioner in Chris's office. Can you please help him if he needs anything?"

"Sure," Maggie forced.

Phil strode across the office and opened the door to Pastor's inner sanctum. The air conditioner man stepped inside.

Phil turned back to Maggie. "Can you tell me how to find Harmony?"

"Uh ..." Maggie seemed unsure how to answer.

So Pete did. "If she's here, she's probably in the hens' wing, but I wouldn't go down there if I were you."

Maggie looked at Tiny. "Would you mind?"

Tiny jumped up. "I'll go get her."

Maggie looked at Phil. "If she's here, he'll find her. Would you like to have a seat?"

Phil looked at Pete and then back at Maggie. He looked incredibly uncomfortable. "No, thanks. I'll wait in Chris's office," he said, and walked by them both.

The air conditioner man stepped out for a minute and returned with a dolly pushing a large unmarked cardboard box.

"Who installs an air conditioner in the fall in Maine?" Pete asked, incredulous.

Maggie just shrugged.

By the time Tiny brought Harmony back to the office, Maggie was off trying to find some laundry soap. So she missed the fireworks. When she returned, Harmony was sitting in Maggie's chair crying, and Tiny was standing over her looking awkward and helpless.

"What happened?" Maggie asked.

"They kicked us out!" Harmony said through clenched teeth. She looked equally heartbroken and furious.

Maggie knelt in front of her longtime friend and looked her in the eye. "Who kicked who out?"

"*They*," Harmony repeated as if that said it all. "The pastor, the elders, *they* have decided that me and Daniel have to leave."

"What? Why?"

"They said Daniel isn't good for the church, isn't good for the image of the church or something. They said he's not really a healer, and they can't be liable for the claims he's made to be one."

Maggie scrunched up her face. "But I don't think he *has* made any claims, has he?"

"Of course not. It's all a bunch of bull. Phil just used a bunch of big words to try to confuse me. He said it all with a smile on his face, like that was going to fool me or something. I hate them." Harmony reached past Maggie's arm to grab a tissue. Then she wiped her eyes, smearing mascara and black eyeliner in every direction. She blew her nose into the blackened tissue. "I'm going to kill them," she said matter-of-factly.

"Shh, don't say that, honey," Maggie said, standing up. "Go get your things. I'll take you to my place. We'll figure this out. They can't just kick you out."

"They can do whatever they want to, and if you take me to your house, your husband is going to freak."

"No he won't. He'll understand."

Harmony looked doubtful.

"Just go get your things. Get Daniel."

Harmony went.

"Should I go with her?" Tiny asked.

"Yeah, that might be a good idea," Maggie said, "though I'm not sure who you'd be protecting, her, or the elders."

"The elder left," he said.

"OK then. Sure, go give her a hand. She might need help lugging her stuff."

Tiny disappeared. Maggie dialed Chris's cell number. It went straight to voicemail. "Hi, Chris," Maggie said with ample snark. "This is Maggie calling from the church. There seems to be some confusion. Can you please call me back and help me clear it up?" She recited her cell number and the church phone too, though he should have long known both those numbers.

Maggie went in first.

Galen had his head under a hood. He looked up when he heard the door shut behind her. "Oh, hey," he said, coming around the Dodge Dart and walking toward her. "You're home early." He gave her a peck on the lips. "Everything OK?"

"Sort of. The good news is Pete's back, but he seems to know exactly who his anonymous friend is. The bad news is, he still doesn't have any glasses."

"Oh shoot, I kind of forgot about that."

"Yeah, me too," Maggie admitted.

"I suppose we could get him some new ones."

"Good grief, Pete's expensive," Maggie said, half-joking.

"It's OK. This car here," he nodded at the car beside him, "needs a lot of work, so that will bring in some cash, and we can put the electric bill off another week."

"OK, but it's going to be hard to fix cars without electricity."

"Oh bosh," Galen said and started to get back to work. Then he paused and looked at his wife, who was still standing there awkwardly. "There's more bad news, isn't there?"

She stood there staring at him as if she was trying to decide what to say. "So Harmony and Daniel are out in the car."

Galen glanced through the window, even though he couldn't see the car from where they were standing. "They are, huh? Why?"

"Well, they just sorta got kicked out of the shelter."

Galen looked at her, his mouth open and eyes wide.

"But it's only temporary. We'll figure it out. I've already called Chris, and—"

"*What's* only temporary? Maggie, what did you tell them?"

Maggie took a deep breath. "This isn't just anyone, Galen. This is Harmony and Daniel we're talking about. My best friend. Our boys' best friend. And it might only be for one night. It might not even be overnight. I just needed someplace to bring them, so they would feel safe and loved while we figure this out."

Galen took a step back from his wife and leaned back on the Dodge. He crossed his arms. "Honey, it's not like I don't love them. But we've been over this. We *have* to have boundaries. We do not live at that church. We live here. We have to put our family first."

"Galen, these people *are* our family."

Galen stared out the window again, his arms still crossed. Maggie shifted her weight from side to side, waiting.

"Why'd they get kicked out?" he asked without looking at her.

"Apparently they said Daniel was bad for the church. Something about liability."

He looked at her. "You're kidding."

She shook her head.

Finally, he dropped his arms and walked back toward the front of the car. "Fine. But tell them it's only for one night. She can take the couch. Daniel can sleep in the boy's room. We'll tell the boys it's a sleepover. Do *not* drag them into this."

That night they made popcorn and watched *Facing the Giants*. All three boys fell asleep before it was over, and Galen dutifully carried each of them to bed. Maggie tucked Harmony in on the couch and then climbed into bed and waited for Galen. He didn't take long to join her. When he did, she snuggled up to him and laid her head on his chest.

"They can't stay here," he whispered, stroking her hair.

"I know," she whispered back and closed her eyes. She was almost asleep when she added, "Thank you."

Several hours later, Maggie woke up and picked up her phone from its charging pad on the nightstand. It was just after one in the morning. She turned and looked at the other side of the bed. It was empty. She untangled herself from her blankets and got out of bed.

The kitchen light was on, and was spilling a thin shaft of light into the bedroom. She followed the light and found Galen sitting at the table, hunched over an open Bible. When he saw her coming, he closed the Bible with a discouraged sigh and leaned back in his chair, causing his back to pop like bubble wrap.

She walked over to him and stopped behind his chair. She began to massage his shoulders and neck, and asked, "Can't sleep?"

He sighed again. "I feel like there's no time to sleep. I need to do something. I need to fix this. I just don't know how. And God won't tell me."

Maggie was silent as she absorbed his words. Then she wordlessly leaned over him and opened his Bible back up. "Just keep listening," she whispered in his ear.

He smiled. "Sure, sure." He closed his eyes and rubbed them.

"Maybe you should sleep on it. Come back to bed."

"I just don't understand how everything has gone so wrong so fast," he said, completely ignoring her suggestion. "God has been protecting the place all these years, and then Dan dies and the devil takes over? Does that make sense to you?" he asked without looking at her.

She didn't answer.

He paused for a beat and then continued. "I get that Dan was special, but he was just a man. I mean, what did he do to keep the house standing?"

Maggie stopped rubbing and perched on the edge of the kitchen table. She looked at her husband's tired face. "I honestly don't know. Maybe the shelter has run its course. Maybe God has accomplished what he wanted to accomplish there."

"And what about Pete? Annie? Tiny? What about Daniel? Look, I can't have Harmony and Daniel living in my house. I love them, but this is my home. This is not a homeless shelter. I have to put my family first."

Maggie didn't respond at first. She just sat there looking at her hands. Galen was quiet too, lost in thought. And Harmony was awake, on the couch, waiting to hear what came next.

"We can't just throw them out," Maggie said.

"I know, honey. But they can't stay here either."

Suddenly, a faint smile appeared on Maggie's face.

"Why on earth are you smiling?" Galen asked, sounding more exhausted than critical.

Her smile grew. "Sorry, I was just thinking about Pastor Dan. Gosh, I loved him. Maybe it was easier for him because he didn't have his own children to worry about, to protect. I can just picture him out there in the morning, his hands up in the air, not caring at all what anyone thought—just him and God."

"What are you talking about?"

"You know, in the morning, when he would pray. He would always keep his hands in the air."

Galen was quiet.

She looked up at him.

"Still don't know what you're talking about. Praying where?"

"You know, in the morning. First thing, before he even had his coffee, he would go out and walk the perimeter, around the whole property, praying for protection, praying for favor, praying for God's will, and whatever needs we had at the time. And he always kept his hands pointed toward heaven."

"I didn't know that."

She looked back down at her hands again. Her smile faded. "Yeah, I used to think it so strange when I first got there, but now, I just wish I could see it again. It was … beautiful."

Galen stood up suddenly. The sound of the chair scraping across the floor as he pushed it back sounded incredibly loud in the nighttime quiet. He headed toward the door.

"What are you doing?"

He opened the door.

"I'm going to go walk around the church and pray. With my hands in the air."

"Now?" Maggie asked, incredulous.

"Yep."

"It's pitch black out there!"

"I'll wear a headlamp."

Chapter 12

Tuesday morning, Pete walked into the salon. "They're finally gone. So, what do you think of my new glasses?"

Maggie looked up and smiled. "They look fantastic."

Pete stuck his hip out in a silly supermodel pose and pointed at his glasses.

Maggie laughed.

"Thank ya very much," Pete said in his Elvis voice. "Your good husband G took me to the mall and got me these fantastic frames. Don't I look smart? Don't suppose I could get a new haircut to go with the new glasses? This stuff on the sides is ruining my look."

Maggie patted the chair. "Have a seat. So Pastor left, huh?"

"Don't you know? Aren't you his secretary?" he said, his voice adrip with sarcasm.

"That'll be enough out of you. I guess I did know he was leaving sometime today. Who'd he end up taking with him?"

Pete sat down. "Just Dwight. I guess Dwight was the only success story." As Pete said "success story," he made air quotes around the words. "All I know is it's going to be so nice with both of them gone."

"Now, behave yourself," Maggie tried.

"That dude's cray cray," Pete said.

"Which dude?"

"Dwight of course. I don't think Chris is crazy. I don't even think he's a bad guy. He's pretty smart. Preaches good. I just don't think he should be working with the homeless. He doesn't *like* us."

"I think he's a bad guy," Tiny offered from the couch, where he was looking at a comic book.

"Anyway," Pete continued, "Dwight is certifiable. I mean, talking to himself nuts."

"What does he say?" Maggie asked.

"I don't know. I don't want to know. I'm just telling you not to be alone with that guy."

"Don't worry, Pete. Tiny and I have that covered." Tiny looked up. Maggie smiled at him. Tiny blushed.

Gertrude appeared in the doorway just then.

"Oh, hey, Gert," Maggie said.

"Do you have an opening?" Gertrude asked. Gertrude and Maggie were old friends. They had been in the shelter together when they were both homeless. Since then, Gertrude had gotten her own place, but she still came for the occasional snip or worship service.

"For you, always," Maggie said, "if you don't mind hanging out for a few minutes while I finish up with Pete here."

"Sure thing," Gertrude said and plopped down on the sofa. "So who is cray cray?"

"Geesh, Gertrude," Pete said, "you got the room bugged or somethin'?"

"Nope. Sound carries. I could hear you flibbertigibbets clear down the hall. So, who's cray cray?"

"What did she just call us?" Pete asked.

Maggie rolled her eyes. "I have no idea. Some Gertrudism. Either way, we probably shouldn't be calling anyone cray cray. And we were talking about a guest here. He's a new believer and he's going through some stuff."

Pete snorted. "Yeah, stuff all right."

"Like what?" Gertrude prodded.

"Let it go, Gert," Maggie tried.

"Not in my nature," Gertrude said. "So what's the deal with this guy?"

"He's some kind of war hero, and it apparently did some damage to his psyche," Pete said.

"Wait a minute. Is this the guy you had on TV? The one who went down front, and the new pastor made such a big deal of it?"

"That's the one," Maggie said. "You watch the show?"

"Sure do! Then I can worship with my cats! Anyway, that guy's not a soldier," Gertrude said casually, while picking up an old magazine from the coffee table in front of her.

Maggie stopped snipping and looked up at her.

Pete stared at her too.

"What do you mean?" Tiny asked.

"What do you think I mean? How do you know he's what he says he is? Is this just like Melanie was once on American Idol, and Duke was an all-star wrestler, and Chief is really from Kansas City? Come on, Chief's never even left Somerset County. And this guy is no soldier. I could tell by the way he held himself. Bad posture."

The room was quiet.

Finally, Maggie said, "Hmm. I guess I never really thought about it. I just believed him when he told me. Maybe I'm just a sucker."

"Nah, Maggie, I think it's true," Pete said. "I mean Pastor wouldn't be dragging him all over the countryside if the guy was a liar? And Gertrude, you can't judge a guy based on his posture."

Gertrude looked serious. "I've caught criminals based on less!"

Pete rolled his eyes. "Oh I forgot, Gertrude the big detective. My bad."

Maggie poked him, hard, in the back.

"Ow!"

"So," Gertrude continued, "can that kid really heal people? Harmony's little boy?"

"God can really heal people," Maggie said.

Suddenly the three of them heard someone running down the hall. Annie appeared in the doorway, her face flushed. "Maggie," she said, out of breath, "call the cops!"

"Oh, now what?" Maggie asked, setting down her scissors.

"There's a huge fight. Chief dumped out a bunch of beer and booze," Annie said, stepping to the side to let Tiny out of the salon so he could go investigate.

"And that's a police matter?"

"No, you don't understand! They're all trying to kill Chief!" Pete ripped his cape off and followed Tiny.

Gertrude got up and wordlessly took his spot.

Maggie did whip out her phone and make the 911 call. Then she shook Pete's cape off and draped it over Gertrude.

"You're not going to go investigate?" Gertrude asked.

"What on earth am I going to do? I'll stay here, where I have weapons. The police will be here soon." Maggie picked up her shears.

Gertrude looked at Maggie in the mirror. "Not sure you're going to do much fighting with those teeny, little things."

Maggie smiled. "I have bigger scissors in the back. Plus, my curling iron is wicked hot."

In less than a minute, the two women heard the sirens.

Pete met the police at the door and showed them the way to the men's quarters, though nearly every police officer in the county knew the layout of the church pretty well by now.

The first officer stepped into the room. Two men were holding Chief to the floor, but they didn't need to be. All the fight seemed to have gone out of him. A third man, Fred, one bloody fist poised to do even more damage, straddled Chief's limp body. "State Police! Stop! Move away from that man."

The men did as they were told.

"Get on your knees, all three of you. You, you too. Get on your knees. Put your hands behind your back." As he put the first offender in cuffs, the second officer knelt beside Chief.

"Hang on, sir," he said, "the ambulance is right behind us."

And it was. Two EMTs rushed into the room, and then immediately one of them turned around to fetch the stretcher. The one who stayed, a petite but feisty-looking female, checked Chief's vitals. She took the stethoscope out of her ears and smiled at his puffy, closed eyes. "Your heart sounds good. You must be as tough as you look. Hang in there." The other EMT, a red-haired male wearing bright orange New Balance tennis shoes that almost matched his head, returned with the stretcher, and they briskly loaded Chief onto the stretcher and then carried him out to the ambulance.

"Need a hand?" Tiny asked as they went by.

The male EMT looked amused. The woman looked annoyed. "No, thanks," she grunted as she went by.

While one police officer gathered statements, the other escorted the offenders out to the cruisers, one by one. They called for a third car for the third suspect.

Tiny volunteered to give the first statement, but the officer made him wait his turn. Once he had shared all that he knew, which was very little, he rushed back to Maggie.

He found her, alone in her salon, cleaning up.

"Well?" she said, looking up. She sounded tired.

"While the guys weren't around, Chief gathered up everybody's alcohol and dumped it in the sink. People were mad."

"I'll bet they were. I'm sure that was a lot of money."

"I don't think that's why they were mad."

"Is Chief OK?" Maggie asked.

"Dunno. They took him away in an ambulance."

Maggie stopped what she was doing. "Seriously? Was he in that bad of shape?"

Tiny shrugged.

Maggie sighed. "I suppose I should call our fearless pastor, huh?"

Tiny shrugged again.

A news van showed up about an hour later. The pretty reporter climbed out of the van, wearing a short skirt and long heels, and she found no shortage of men willing to talk to her. And they provided her with several completely unreliable, conflicting stories:

"Chief started it. They arrested the wrong guy."

"Chief stole a bunch of money."

"Someone stole some money from Chief."

"Chief was stealing everybody's food and beer."

"Chief was sleeping with Aaron's sister."

It seemed that the new, unimproved Open Door Church just couldn't seem to stay out of the limelight.

At Bible study that night, Galen opened with Matthew 5:38-41. He read it slowly, and then stopped and looked at his congregants. His efforts were met with blank stares.

He read the Scripture again. Then he asked Tiny to come up front to join him. Tiny did as he was asked. "Whatever you do," he mumbled to Tiny, "do *not* hit me."

Tiny, taking whatever task was about to be his completely seriously, nodded. "OK."

"Now," Galen said to his reluctant audience, "what do you think Jesus meant by 'turn the other cheek'?" Galen didn't wait for an answer. "If I hit Tiny, and I realize, that would not be a wise thing to do, but if I hit Tiny like this ..." Galen mimed a right hook to Tiny's left cheek. "Then Jesus is telling Tiny that he wants him to ..." Tiny didn't even wait for the words. He immediately turned his right cheek toward Galen. "That's right, Tiny. Good. Jesus wants Tiny to turn his other cheek to me, to offer his other cheek to me also." He paused for a few seconds, and then said, "Thanks, Tiny. You can go sit down." He continued, "Jesus doesn't say this because he wants us to get punched, but he's showing us how to *submit* to each other. He's showing us that you"—he pointed at Randy—"don't always have to be right. That you"—he pointed at Kevin—"don't have to avenge everything." He pointed at Annie. "That this life is not about *you* ..." He looked at Bev. "Or *you*." He looked at Joyce. "Or *you*. It's not about me. Or my beautiful wife. Or my amazing kids. It's not about any of us. If someone steals your shirt, you *then hand them your coat too*. This is how our founder, Pastor Dan, lived. This is how Jesus lived and continues to live through people like Pastor Dan.

"Folks, what happened here today is unacceptable. Whether you all choose to believe in Jesus or not, it is his love, his power, his resurrection that made this place possible, that brought me here, that brought my wife here—it was Jesus who put this roof over your head. So you might want to pay a little more attention to his teaching. Because none of this is guaranteed." Galen stopped and looked around the room. "All of this"—he spread his arms out—"could be gone tomorrow. *You* could be gone tomorrow."

Chapter 13

Shortly after noon on Wednesday, Galen was out rescuing someone with the tow truck, Maggie was working at the church, the boys were all still in school, and Harmony was sunning herself on the hood of a car that was parked beside Galen's garage.

Elder Phil pulled into the drive. Harmony looked up at him, and then lay back down. "G's not here," she called as he got out of his car.

"I can see that. Don't think he'd appreciate you showing so much skin in his yard."

Harmony looked up sharply, seeming to recognize something in his tone. "There's no one around to see this skin. We're in the middle of nowhere. What do you want?"

"A little chilly for sunbathing, don't you think?" he asked, walking toward her.

Harmony put her head back down and covered her eyes with an arm. "Just trying to get some sun before it dies for the winter. Like I said, what do you want?"

"I just wanted to talk to you about this unfortunate event."

"Which one?" She appeared to be disinterested, but her arms had broken out in gooseflesh.

Phil leaned against the car, his body close to Harmony's, but his gaze staring off into the distance. "I don't think you should have been asked to leave the shelter," he said softly.

She looked at the back of his head. "Um, I wasn't exactly *asked*, and weren't you the one who told me to pack?"

"Well, it's possible we were wrong. It's not your fault, all this business about your boy. In fact, I'd like to help, if you'd like that."

"If I'd like it? What are you going to do to help?"

He turned to her then, still leaning against the car, his weight now mostly on his elbow, and his face less than a foot from hers. "Well, the thing is Harmony, you're a beautiful woman, and well, I could be persuaded, if you'd like, to talk to the elders about getting you back into the shelter."

Harmony leaned in closer to him. "Really?"

"Sure could. The only thing is, well, you'd have to tell your boy to stop praying for people in public, stop trying to heal them. Then this can all go away." He leaned even closer to her, his face now inches from hers, and he lightly dragged one fingertip down her arm. "What do you think about that?"

"I think you should come inside," Harmony said, and swung her long, bare legs off the car's hood.

Harmony was back at the church an hour later. Maggie saw her walk by the office window, a bag slung over each arm. "Hey, Harm!" Maggie called out.

Harmony backpedaled to look at Maggie through the open doorway. "Yeah?"

"Whatcha doin'?"

"What's it look like?"

Maggie frowned. "It looks like you're moving back in."

"Well, that's 'cause I am. Mind your own business, Maggie," Harmony said tonelessly, and then continued down the hall.

When Galen returned to an empty house, he found a note: "Gone back to church. It's all good. Thanks for everything."

On Saturday, when Pastor pulled his new truck into the church parking lot, the guests scattered like rabbits to their holes.

Dwight practically strutted through the front door. "Welcome home," Maggie said, sounding almost welcoming as she did so.

Dwight did not respond, only sneered as he brushed by her.

Chris had a job for her, though. "Hi, Maggie," he said brightly as he came through the door. "How has your week been?"

"Good," Maggie said, sounding cautious.

"That's great. We had a fantastic time too. Really got a lot of good publicity for the church, and I've booked several other speaking engagements with churches up and down the east coast." He handed Maggie a piece of paper with a list of dates and church names. "Could you please find a hotel for Dwight and me in each of these cities on these dates? Then let me see the list, and once I approve it, I'll give you the church credit card and you can make the reservations for me. Thanks a lot." He walked by her, as she stood speechless, still holding the list out in front of her. He'd only taken a few steps when he stopped, turned around, and added, "Oh, and could you also fix up one of the empty family rooms for Dwight?"

Maggie turned around slowly to face him. "For Dwight? Why?"

"Things just aren't working out for him in the larger sleeping area." He turned again and left Maggie standing in the hallway.

Pete came out of the office. "What was that all about?"

Maggie didn't look at Pete. Her face stayed slack, her eyes focused on Chris walking away. "Um, not really sure?" It wasn't until Chris was out of her sight, around the bend in the hallway, that she finally looked at Pete. "Uh, could you put some clean sheets in one of the empty family rooms? Just one set."

This was a strange request, and Pete looked appropriately confused. "Just one bed? OK, you want me to make it up?"

"No. Definitely not. He can make his own bed." And with that, Maggie carried her list of speaking engagements into the office, leaving Pete standing in the hallway, alone with his confusion.

Maggie was only a third of the way through the hotel list when Chris returned to the office. She looked up at him, and there was pent-up fury in her eyes. "You know, this isn't really my job."

He put on a diplomatic smile and looked around the office. "Oh sorry, are you busy?"

Maggie wasn't busy, at the moment, and she didn't answer him, just continued with her fiery glare.

He continued, "I *can* do that myself, but I'm just very busy, got appointments all day, and I would appreciate it so much if you could help with the operational details."

Maggie squinted. "Are you trying to trick me into thinking that you're doing me some sort of favor by letting me be such a big part of your big, fancy operation around here? Just what do you do all day? You're always off to some meeting. Who do you meet with? 'Cause it's certainly not homeless people."

Chris sighed. He looked around the office, as if to confirm they were alone, and then pulled Tiny's chair closer to Maggie's desk. He sat and leaned forward on his knees. "Look, Maggie. I'm doing my best here. I really am. This is all new to me. I'm just trying to do the best I can, but I can't be everywhere at once. I am meeting with other pastors in the area, trying to garner their support, both prayer support and financial. I am meeting with local leaders, trying to garner their favor, trying to undo some of the negative reputation that this church has. This position is about more than preaching on Sundays. It's about making this institution into all it can be. I am the public face of Open Door now." His phone vibrated inside his jacket. He took it out and looked at it. "If you'll excuse me," he said without looking at Maggie, "I've got to take this." He got up, went into his office, and closed the door.

The next morning, Pastor Chris welcomed everyone to the service. "Good morning! Welcome to the homeless here with us, to our loyal members here with us, and to all those joining us from home. We are glad you could be with us today."

There were several audible groans from the homeless there with him.

"What loyal members?" Cari mumbled to Maggie. "Mike and Lisa have stopped coming. I think it's just the three of us now." She began singing "Just the Two of Us," only changing the lyric to just the "three" of us.

Maggie giggled, and Galen gave them both a stern look.

"Don't forget Gertrude," Maggie whispered.

"Just the *four* of us," Cari sang.

"Shh!" Galen said.

Chris was still talking: "Dwight Schultz, our Iraq War veteran, and myself, have just returned from the New England Pastors' Convention in Springfield, Massachusetts, where we shared about our ministry to the homeless with thousands of pastors and church leaders from all denominations and all over the country. What a blessed time it was! As Dwight shared his testimony of how he came to know Jesus as Savior through this ministry, I don't dare say there was a dry eye in the house! And as a result, I have been invited to speak in churches all over New England. And I'm ready for the challenge! If those of you joining us from home know of a church or ministry that would like to improve its outreach to the homeless, please, give me a call! God is moving, friends! God has not forgotten our homeless brothers and sisters! He is equipping us to reach them, and reach them we must! The Great Commission does not exclude those who are sleeping in alleys and on park benches! They need Christ too! Let us pray."

The following week, there was more mail than ever. But Maggie didn't open any of it. She just made a big pile of it on the floor outside of Chris's locked door.

Chapter 14

On Friday morning, Maggie walked into the church to find Tiny standing by the locked office door with two cups of coffee in his hands. This was not unusual. The look on his face was.

"Tiny, what's wrong?" Maggie asked.

"I didn't do it," Tiny said.

"OK. Didn't do what?" Maggie took one of the cups of coffee out of his hand. "Thank you."

He nodded.

Maggie fiddled with her keys to find the right one, but when she did, she noticed that the office door had been forced open. It was shut now, but it was obvious that a crowbar had recently done some damage to both the cheap door and the ancient door frame. She gently pushed on the door and it swung open. And then she gasped.

The office had been destroyed. Every drawer had been opened and papers and books lay all over the floor. She set her coffee down on her desk and moaned. Her computer was gone. The closet door had been forced open, but the thieves had apparently learned what she already knew—there wasn't much in there to steal, unless one really wanted a neon orange softball cap from eons gone by.

"I'll help you pick up," Tiny said.

"Thank you, Tiny."

She looked around the room and saw that Chris's door had also been forced open. It still stood ajar. She walked through it. His office was in worse shape than hers. His computer was gone too. His framed degree now lay on the floor, the thin, cracked glass bearing what was probably a footprint. His bookshelf had been tipped over, his drawers ransacked, his window busted out.

"Wait," Maggie said. "I thought they came in through the office. Why'd they break the window?"

"I think they did that to get the safe out," Tiny said.

"What safe?" Maggie looked at Tiny. He didn't answer. "What safe, Tiny?"

Tiny looked guilty. She took a step toward him and softened her voice. "Tiny, you didn't do anything wrong. Just tell me, what do you know about a safe?"

"Not much," Tiny said, looking at the floor. "It's just that Dwight was talking, he talks a lot when he drinks, and he was talking about how much money Pastor has, and he said he keeps it in a hidden safe, you know, to keep it safe. And hidden."

Maggie looked around in wonder. "I don't see how that's possible, Tiny. I think Dwight is just spinning tales." Then her eyes landed on a large, empty cabinet, it's door hanging by a single hinge. She sighed. "I'd better call Chris." She took out her phone to dial. As she did, she asked Tiny, "Have you heard anything else? Do you know if anyone saw or heard anything?"

"No," Tiny said, "but maybe G saw something when he was praying this morning?"

Maggie thought about that for a second. "Maybe. Maybe not, though. This wall is next to the parsonage wall. I'm pretty sure he walks around the whole property, without cutting between the buildings. But we can ask him."

Chris's phone went to voicemail. "Hey, Chris, it's Maggie. Look, you'd better get down here. Someone has broken into your office. They took your computer. Not sure what else. I'll call the police." She hung up and dialed the police. She had them on speed dial. They said they would send an officer right out. Just as she was hanging up with them, Chris called her back.

"Hello?"

"Whatever you do, don't call the police!" Chris barked.

"What? Why?"

"Because ... because, we don't need bad publicity. People will be scared to stay there if they think it's not safe. And our insurance is going to go up. Just do as I say! I'll be right there!" He hung up, not giving her a chance to tell him that the police were already on their way.

In fact, they beat him to the church. Two officers, in two separate cars, were there within minutes. They took photos, and were beginning to question the guests when Chris finally arrived.

He took one step into his office and his hands flew to his head. "Oh, no ... oh, no," he moaned.

"Pastor?" one of the officers asked. "Can you answer a few questions?"

Chris didn't respond.

"Pastor?" the officer repeated.

"What?" Chris snapped.

"We're trying to figure out how the thieves got into the building. Who has a key?"

"Just myself and the elders," Chris said, thoughtfully. Then he gave Maggie a dirty look. "And her."

"It's all the same key," Maggie said. "If someone had a key for the outside door, they would have just used it on the office door too, instead of prying it open."

The other officer spoke up. "There's a window in the sanctuary that is wide open. Could have been left like that, or they could have gotten it open somehow. Could've come in that way."

"Well, then why didn't they just use that window?" Chris said, nodding at the smashed window in his office.

"The fact that they didn't come in your window," said the first officer, "suggests it was an outside job. It was probably someone who didn't know the layout of the building—"

"Or someone who was already inside when the doors were locked," Chris interrupted.

"It wasn't one of our guests, Chris!" Maggie argued.

"OK," the officer redirected them, "can you tell us if anything is missing? Other than your computer? Mrs. Turney has already told us that your desktop has been stolen."

"No," Chris said without looking around. "I'm sure nothing else was taken. There was nothing else to steal."

"What about the safe?" the officer asked.

"What safe?" Chris snapped.

"OK then," the officer said, writing some notes, "but Mr. uh …" He looked up at Tiny. "… Tiny here says that there was a safe in your office—"

"Well, *Tiny* is a *huge* idiot," Chris spat, "who has never even been in my office. Now if you don't mind, can you please clear out? I've got some cleaning up to do. And we won't be filing any sort of report, so you can go."

"I'm sorry, Pastor, but there will be a report. Mrs. Turney here has reported several things stolen, so we have to investigate."

Chris looked around till he saw Maggie, and then shot daggers at her with his eyes. "And just what pray tell, was stolen from *you?*"

Completely phlegmatically, Maggie replied, "My sunglasses, two lipsticks, and an envelope full of money. It also appears that they've taken your new air conditioner."

Chris sneered. "*You* had an envelope full of money in the church office? Why?"

"Well, you took away the slush fund, so I had a little emergency cash, you know, in case someone needed a Band-Aid and I didn't want to take the time to fill out a purchase order."

The police officer looked back and forth between them as if sensing that he should interrupt their discourse, but also fearing to do so.

Galen walked in just then and crossed the room quickly to his wife. "Why didn't you call me?" he asked, taking her into his arms.

"I'm fine. No one was hurt. It's fine. How did you know?"

"Pete called me."

"It happened last night," Maggie said. "Did you see anything when you walked the perimeter this morning?"

"Aw shoot. No, I didn't. I'm usually looking directly in front of my feet. It was still pretty dark this morning when I was out there." Galen looked at the police officer. "Sorry, I didn't see a thing."

"Why were you walking around in the dark this morning?" Chris snapped.

"I was praying."

"Praying for what?"

Without hesitation, Galen replied, "For you."

Pastor glared at Galen for several speechless seconds, then at Maggie, and then finally stormed out of the office.

"Wow, nice guy," the cop muttered.

"He's trying," Galen said. "I think." Then he looked down at his wife. "Do you just want to go home?"

She nodded. "Definitely."

Galen led her back outside. Before she got into the car, she finally took a sip of the coffee Tiny had gotten for her. It was lukewarm, and she dumped it out into the dirt.

Pastor Chris returned to his office with Dwight in tow. They waited as the police finished working, and then the police left, and Chris and Dwight began to put the office back together. It took them all day.

Maggie didn't return to church that day, so she wasn't there to hear her best friend's pained gasp just as Galen called the Bible study to order.

Galen did hear Harmony, and followed her eyes to the doorway. At first, he didn't seem to recognize the person standing in it. Then obvious recognition, and dismay, fell over his face. "You've *got* to be kidding me," he muttered. Then he looked around the room and seemed to remember that dozens of people were staring at him, waiting for him to begin. "Welcome, everyone. If you would, please turn your Bibles to Psalm 68." A few people opened their personal Bibles. Some reached for pew Bibles. Others ignored Galen entirely. He waited as the sound of flipping pages filled the otherwise quiet. "Psalms is the longest book in the Bible," Galen said. "And it's right in the middle of the Bible, so if you open your Bible to the center, you might well land in Psalms." There was some more page flipping and then the sound settled down. As it did, the newcomer settled into an aisle seat near the back. Looking pale, Harmony had also turned back around to face Galen. He made eye contact with her, and his eyes were full of compassion.

"OK, so this psalm is actually a song written by King David. As many of you know, King David was one of the major players in the Bible. He was an ancestor of Jesus, and he was a mighty leader who truly loved God. So, in verses five and six, King David writes about God, 'Father of the fatherless and a judge for the widows is God in his holy habitation. God makes a home for the lonely.'" Galen set his Bible down and paused, looking at the people in front of him. He was not behind the pulpit. He wasn't even on the stage. He was standing immediately in front of the front pew. He didn't even have a microphone. He was wearing an old Skillet T-shirt and stained blue jeans. "Friends, nowhere in the Bible does it suggest that God is impressed by people who live flashy lives. God's heart is with people who are lonely in this lifetime. But I promise you, if you give your lives to God, if you give your hearts to God, you won't be lonely anymore. He is making a home for you. He has given you a home here, but this is only temporary. It's not a perfect home." There were some chuckles.

"Ain't that the truth," Randy offered.

"But God is also making you a perfect home that is not temporary. Friends, this life is not about *this* life. It's about eternity. And I want to give you a quick history lesson here. Don't tune me out. This is important. In this verse, King David uses a simple Hebrew word, *'ab*, which our Bible translates to the English 'father.' But in the Hebrew that King David originally used, this was a very simple word, a word that little children used to refer to their human fathers. It's an easy word to say, and is one of the very first words that Hebrew children are able to pronounce to this day. It's more like the way we use our word 'daddy' than it is the way we use the word 'father.' King David uses this simple word for an all-powerful God. This means that you can have a very personal, a very real, a very special relationship with the almighty God. God is the God of the universe, but he is also your daddy. I know some of you don't have human fathers. God is your father. I know some of you don't have homes. God is your home. He is your shelter, and he is everything you need. If you just let him, he will take care of you. God loves his children, better than any human father ever can." Galen paused and looked at the man in the back, the man who had just joined them for the first time in more than eight years, the man who had left his girlfriend without a word, the man named Levi who had never even met his biological son, Daniel.

Galen then looked back at his own people. "If any of you have any questions, I will try to answer them."

Annie raised her hand.

"Yes, Annie?"

"If God loves me so much, why did he ever allow me to be fatherless in the first place? I've never even met my father and my mother never gave a crap about me."

"That's a good question, Annie, and one that I bet other people here have. I can't speak for God, but I can tell you that God allows us to go through hard things, because if we didn't go through hard things, we would never understand that we need God. We would think we could do everything ourselves. Does that make sense?"

Annie nodded, looking at least partially satisfied.

"Are there any other questions?"

No one else moved.

"OK then, let's close in prayer." Galen prayed over his friends and asked God to protect them and keep their hearts safe. When he said "amen," the people scattered, and Levi made his way toward

Harmony. Galen got to her first. "Just tell me what you need me to do," he whispered to her.

"Get Daniel out of here," she said, and placed the little boy's hand into Galen's large, protective one. Daniel looked surprised, but also completely trusting.

"Come on, bud. Let's go to the kitchen and see if there's any ice cream."

Daniel followed Galen obediently, but said, "The kitchen's locked at night."

"Don't worry, I have a master key," Galen said, and they were out of the sanctuary and headed toward the stairs.

"Does Pastor Chris know that?" Daniel asked, and Galen laughed.

"What do you want?" Harmony asked Levi.

"I wanted to see you," Levi said, reaching for her hand.

Harmony yanked it away and swore at him. "Don't touch me. Don't you dare. You can just go. Get out of here."

"I want to see my son."

"You don't have a son," Harmony spat.

"Yes I do, and I want to see him."

"You don't have a son," Harmony repeated.

Levi's jaw tightened, and his hands clenched into fists. "Look, you can't stop me from seeing my son."

Harmony turned to go, and Levi grabbed her arm and yanked her toward him.

"Let go of me!" Harmony yelled.

"I know he's mine, Harmony. I saw him on the news. It said he'd grown up in the shelter. Wasn't hard to do the math. So I come back to this dump and there he is sitting snuggled right up to you. Now where did he go?"

Harmony slapped him across the face, hard. He didn't look surprised, just angry. He grabbed the offending arm with his free hand and now had her by both arms, squeezing hard enough to hurt.

"Take your hands off her," Galen said from behind.

Levi craned his neck around. "Or what?"

Galen advanced so quickly that Levi dropped his grip. "You need to leave," Galen said.

"Where's the kid?" Levi asked.

Harmony looked alarmed, as if she was wondering the same thing.

"He's eating ice cream with Tiny. In other words, it would be physically impossible for you to get to him. So you should go."

"He's my kid. You can't keep him away from me."

"OK. Then you pay for the lawyer and you pay for the paternity test and then we'll do what the judge says. Until then, get off this property and don't come back."

Levi looked from Galen's face to Harmony's and back to Galen's. Then, grudgingly, he stalked toward the door, trying to look tough as he went.

Harmony's eyes filled with tears. "What am I going to do?"

"Get your stuff. You're moving back to my place."

Harmony went to her room to pack, and Galen went to get Daniel.

"Thanks, Tiny," Galen said, patting Tiny on the back.

"No problem. I like ice cream," Tiny said.

Galen waited patiently for Daniel to finish his Moose Tracks. Then, when Daniel started to lick out the bowl, Galen said, "OK, little man. Finish up. We're going back to my house for a sleepover."

"Was that my father?" Daniel asked.

Galen's face fell. "What makes you ask that?"

Daniel shrugged. He took another lick. "I dunno. Just knew."

"Well, you'll have to talk to your mother about it. But for now, let's get you to my place."

"No, thank you," Daniel said.

Galen's brow furrowed. "What?"

"Thank you, G, for helping, but I don't need to go to your house. We'll be OK here."

Harmony joined them then with a backpack slung over each shoulder. "Come on, Daniel, let's go."

"Mama, we don't need to go. He won't come back."

"What? Who won't come back?"

"That guy. That man who is my father. He won't come back. God will protect me. Don't worry, Mama. God will protect us. I don't want to go to G's house. I just want to go to bed. I'm tired." He took his exceptionally clean ice cream bowl and spoon to the tray return as Galen and Harmony stood there tongue-tied. Then Daniel headed up the stairs. Halfway up, he turned back toward them. "Thanks for eating ice cream with me, Tiny."

Tiny nodded and waved. He was still eating.

Harmony looked at Galen. "What do I do?"

Galen sighed. "I don't know. What do you want to do?"

"Well, the church will be locked, right?"

Galen looked at his watch. "It's still over an hour till curfew. But then it will be locked."

"OK then. I guess we'll stay." She didn't look so sure, though.

"I could sleep in the hallway, outside the door," Tiny said.

At the same time, Galen said, "You don't have to do that, Tiny," and Harmony said, "That would be great!"

Tiny smiled and stood to tower over them. "I'll go get a pillow." He headed for the stairs, still carrying his treat.

"OK, you call me if you need *anything*," Galen said. "Even if you hear anything suspicious."

Harmony nodded. "Sometimes I wish you guys would just move into the parsonage."

Chapter 15

On Sunday morning, it was as if the break-in had never happened. Chris took the pulpit with aplomb and preached with polish, delivering a sermon on the contrast between Solomon's wisdom and wealth.

"I hate him," Maggie muttered to her husband halfway through the sermon.

Galen looked at her. "Paper?" he whispered.

Maggie looked surprised, then nodded and rummaged through her purse until she came up with a small notebook. She handed it to him.

He took it and then held his open hand out again.

She handed him a pen too.

And he wrote his wife a note in church: "We both need to stop feeling ill will toward the man. He is just a man. He is not the real enemy. God asks us to love him and pray for him. We need to trust God to deal with him. It's not our job." She watched him closely, reading as he wrote, so when he finished, he didn't even need to hand her the note. She sighed and gave him a look that was simultaneously annoyed and acquiescent. Then she gave her attention back to the man behind the pulpit, as Galen gently took his wife's hand in his own.

Toward the end of the sermon, Chris announced, "I will be away next Sunday, and a guest speaker will be filling in for me here. I hate to miss another Sunday at my home church, but I've been invited to speak at First Baptist in Haleyville, Connecticut. They want to hear more about our exciting ministry here, and I will be happy to tell them all about you fine people."

Galen leaned to Maggie's ear and whispered, "Who's the guest speaker?"

Maggie shook her head. "No idea."

As Chris began his benediction, Daniel stood up suddenly. "Excuse me please!"

Harmony said, "Oh no!" and yanked Daniel back into his seat.

Daniel popped right back up again. "Excuse me please, but I know that someone is sick here." He turned and looked at the congregation, his little blue eyes resting on a young woman he didn't know.

"Please, don't," Harmony said, "we can do this later. Not in church!"

Daniel peeled his mother's hand from his arm and walked toward the young woman. "Are you sick?"

She nodded, looking bewildered.

Daniel smiled. "Don't be scared. I'm just going to pray for you. I don't know if it will work, but I think it will." Daniel reached her and knelt in front of her. Then he folded his little hands and bowed his head. The room remained silent for the duration of Daniel's prayer. All eyes, and the cameras, were on him. After a few minutes, Daniel looked up, smiled at the woman and said, "God's will be done." Then he stood up and walked to his seat as Pastor Chris gave the benediction.

As everyone filed out of the sanctuary, Harmony grabbed Daniel's chin and pointed it toward her. "I told you not to do that!" she scolded.

Daniel's eyes maintained his innocence. "Why?"

She let go of his chin. "Because I said so! Because I'm your mother! Because I don't need to explain everything to you!"

Daniel nodded. "I'm sorry, Mama. I had to. God told me to." Then he turned and walked toward the door, his head hanging.

Harmony looked up to see Maggie staring at her. "Don't look at me like that," she snapped.

"Sorry, Harm. But why are you being so hard on him? He's doing a good thing here."

"Can you just stay out of it?" she said, without looking at her friend. She picked up her things and took off after her son.

Maggie, appearing to have no intentions of staying out of anything, followed Harmony. Galen, who had been chatting with someone else, saw his wife leaving. He gathered up his boys, one of whom was about to bust out a drum solo, and took off after her. They caught up with her on her way downstairs. "Are we eating here?" Galen asked.

"Not sure yet, but something's wrong with Harmony. She's been acting off for days."

"OK then, so we're not leaving. Go ahead boys, get some lunch." The boys ran ahead.

Maggie didn't go to the food line. She just sat down at Harmony's usual table, which was empty at that moment. Harmony and Daniel went through the food line, but then Harmony sat down at a different table.

Maggie was undeterred. She got up, walked to Harmony's new table, and plopped down in front of her. "Talk to me."

Harmony looked up. Her eyes were wet. "I can't."

"Why on earth not? Look, I know this must be hard. I have no idea how one is supposed to act when their kid is performing miracles, but let's at least talk about it. We've always talked about everything before."

"It's not that," Harmony said. She put her fork down and looked around. Then she leaned forward a little. "I told him to stop it. I told him he wasn't allowed to heal people in church anymore. And he just did it anyway!"

"But why would you tell him such a thing? What do you think is going to happen? Are you afraid he's going to be exploited or something?"

Harmony rolled her eyes. "I really hate it when you use big words. Can't you just talk like a normal person? I told him that because that's what *Phil* told me."

"Phil Miller?"

"Yep. *Elder* Phil."

"Why?"

"I don't know." Harmony picked up her fork again.

"But why would he want Daniel to stop healing people?" Maggie leaned back, looking perplexed. Harmony, apparently done talking, took a big bite of meatloaf. Maggie beckoned to her husband, who was sitting at Harmony's usual table, seeming to enjoy his own slice of meatloaf. Grudgingly, he got up and came to sit beside his wife.

"Yeah?" he asked as he slid into the metal folding chair beside her.

"Tell him what you told me," Maggie said to Harmony.

Harmony sighed. "Can't you just let it go, Maggie?"

"No."

"So," Harmony said to Galen, "Phil made me promise that Daniel would stop healing people. It was a condition of us moving back here."

"What?!" Maggie exclaimed. "You didn't tell me that! Why? I don't understand."

Galen groaned. "I understand. It's that woman. The one who called Daniel a fraud. The elders are paranoid about our church getting any negative attention."

"We've *always* got negative attention here," Maggie said. "This place is a pitstop for misfits."

Galen guffawed. "Right. We should put that on the sign. Well, anyway, Harmony, let your boy do what God tells him to do. If you get kicked out again, you can sleep on our couch. But I have a feeling God has got more going on here than we understand. I've got a feeling this is much bigger than any of us."

The guest preacher was none other than Elder Albert Pelotte, whom the people living at the church hadn't laid eyes on in more than a month, except for that one time that Tiny claimed he saw Albert stealing several pounds of bacon out of the shelter's fridge, but that was never corroborated.

His message was nothing short of painful, and several of the men actually stretched out on the pews in the back and went to sleep. Normally, Galen would have put a stop to such behavior, but he let it slide this time.

Albert's sermon—if one could even call it that—was all about how rough Albert's life had been, all the hardships he'd been through, but how he had overcome them all—"pulled myself up by my bootstraps," he said. If his point was that he was able to do so by the power of God, he failed to make that clear.

About halfway through the message, Maggie gave Galen a pleading look.

"I think he's trying to inspire them," Galen said quietly.

Maggie snorted, not quietly.

At one point Duke fell so deep into dreamland that he began to snore. At first, this was amusing and far more entertaining than the preaching, so the people around him didn't interfere with his nap. But the longer Albert talked, the louder Duke sawed, and finally, Kevin, who was sitting two rows behind him, stood up and bonked Duke on the head with his cane. This startled Duke awake, and he swore, and everyone laughed, but Albert never missed a beat. He was in his own little world behind the pulpit.

Galen and his family were on their way out the door when Tiny pulled on Maggie's elbow. "What's up, Tiny?"

Tiny turned and walked to the corner of the lobby, looking around furtively as he went.

Maggie followed. "What is it, Tiny?"

Tiny swallowed hard. "Dwight has a gun. I saw it."

"But Dwight's not even here. Didn't he go with Pastor to speak at that other church?"

Tiny nodded, but didn't say anything.

"So you saw the gun this morning?"

Tiny shook his head.

"Well, then when did you see it?" Maggie appeared to be losing her boundless patience with Tiny.

"Wednesday."

"Wednesday?! And you're just telling me now?"

Tiny looked at the floor, his shoulders dropping along with his gaze. "I'm sorry, Maggie. I didn't wanna be no rat. I've been askin' God what I should do, and I think he wants me to tell you."

Maggie sighed. "It's OK, Tiny. You did the right thing. Good job. I'll go call the police. We can't have people having guns in here."

"OK. Thanks, Maggie. Can I go eat my lunch now?"

"Of course." Maggie turned to find Galen, who was still standing where she'd left him. He and his boys were cornered by Gertrude, who apparently had a fairly gripping story to share.

"If you'll excuse me, Gert, I need to speak to my husband."

Galen said goodbye to Gertrude and followed Maggie outside. He held Elijah in his arms and Isaiah trailed behind. "Brrr," Galen said. "It's getting cold out already. Shelter will be filling up soon."

Maggie stopped walking and turned to face him. "Yeah, so apparently Dwight has a gun."

"Oh, you really did need to talk to me. I thought you were just rescuing me from Gertrude."

"Well, that too. Can I use your phone? Mine's dead."

"Why?"

"Why is my phone dead?"

"No." Galen sighed, setting Elijah down on the ground despite his protests. "Who are you going to call?"

"Who do you think? The police, of course."

Galen's brow furrowed.

"What?" Maggie asked.

"I'm not sure we should call the police just yet. I mean, Dwight's not here, right? And I don't even know if it's against the law for him to have a gun."

"It's against our rules!" Maggie said indignantly.

"I'm not sure. Is it?"

Maggie heaved a frustrated sigh. "Fine, Mr. Nice Guy. I'm calling the cops."

"Just calm down—"

Maggie shot him a look that stopped him mid-sentence.

"Sorry, honey. I understand why you're upset. Just give me a few minutes, OK? Don't call the cops yet." He waited for her to agree, which she finally did with a terse nod. He smiled and kissed her on the cheek. Then he trotted back into the church.

Most of the men bunked in one large room. Several years before, a large church in Texas had funded an addition that had more than doubled the size of the church. This large room was part of that addition. Rows and rows of bunk beds made it look like some sort of military barracks. Except the room was very, very messy. For men with no homes, these men managed to consume a *lot* of junk food, and the evidence was everywhere, competing only with dirty laundry for complete dominance of the room.

"Shoot," Galen muttered as soon as he walked in. He looked around as if overwhelmed with the daunting search before him.

Pete came up behind him. "What are you doing here?"

"Ah, good. I could use your help. You wanna tell me which of these bunks is Dwight's?"

Pete laughed. "Oh, his highness doesn't sleep down here with us paupers."

"Paupers?" Galen asked, one eyebrow raised.

"Never mind, come on." Pete turned to head back the way he'd come, beckoning to Galen with one hand. Galen followed Pete down a hallway, up a flight of stairs and down another hallway into the section of the church reserved for families. "This is it," Pete said, pointing to a closed door.

"He lives in here alone?" Galen asked.

Pete nodded.

Galen tried the doorknob. It was locked.

"What did you expect?" Pete asked.

"I didn't expect to have to use my master key," he said, fishing his keyring out of his pocket.

"Do they know you have that?" Pete asked.

Galen unlocked the door and then pushed it open. "That's the second time I've been asked that question this week." He and Pete stayed standing at the threshold, taking it all in.

Pete blew out an impressed puff of air. "I didn't know it was possible for one man to make this big of a mess."

"Me neither," Galen said, taking a tentative step inside.

"Wanna tell me what we're doing here, G? Someone's gonna see us, and if Dwight finds out we were in here, well, I just don't want to deal with that."

"We're looking for a gun. Well, *I'm* looking for a gun. You're welcome to help."

"A gun? Dwight has a gun in here?" He looked around as if that was utterly impossible.

"I don't know. But I'm going to look around," Galen said.

"Look around? It would take you all day to go through this garbage. And he's totally going to know you were in here."

Galen sighed and put his hands on his hips. "I don't know what else to do. I mean, we should have a no-firearms rule, and I'm sure we would have, if Pastor Dan had ever needed one. But I don't think he did."

"What are you planning to do if you find a gun?"

"I'm going to leave it right where it is and call the police," Galen said.

"What? Why not just call the cops now then?"

"Because I don't want to stir up even more drama!" Galen snapped. "Because I'm going on Tiny's word here, and he could have seen a squirt gun for all we know. Because I ... because I ... because I'm trying to do what Dan would have done."

Pete waited to make sure Galen was done talking. Then he said, "You know what I would've done if you were Pastor Dan and we were in this same exact situation?"

"No, what?"

"I would've called the police. And that's what I'm going to do right now. I'll leave Tiny's name out of it, and yours. You get out of this room. We were never here." And without waiting for a reply, Pete vanished down the hall.

One policeman showed up.

"I can't search the room without permission from Pastor ..." He hesitated.

"Pastor Chris?" Galen offered.

"I guess. Is that who's in charge now?"

"Sort of," Galen said, and the cop scowled.

"Yes," Pete said. "Pastor Chris is in charge now, but he's away this weekend."

The three men were standing together in the otherwise empty church lobby. The policeman appeared to want to be anywhere else. "OK, well, who is second in command?"

"I am," Pete lied.

Galen's eyes grew wide, and Pete avoided making eye contact with him.

"I am in charge right now, and we have some people concerned that there is a gun in an unlocked room. It is important that our guests feel safe here."

"OK then. Show me the way."

Pete led the officer down the hallway, and Galen followed along.

Galen had left the door unlocked, so after a quick perfunctory knock, the policeman opened the door. "You two stay out here," the cop said abruptly, and went in.

"You bet," Galen said gratefully and then looked at Pete. "How many lies did you just tell?" he muttered.

Pete shrugged, still not looking at him.

"That's not OK, Pete!"

"I expect to have a lot worse things to answer for when my time comes."

Eventually, Pete and Galen got bored watching the officer poke around, and they went back to the office.

"Maggie is going to wonder what on earth is taking me so long," Galen said, sitting down in her chair.

"Did you send her home?" Pete asked, looking around as if he expected her to pop up from behind a filing cabinet.

"Yeah, as soon as you said you were calling the cops. I figured we'd be here awhile."

"Well, as long as we're waiting, you wanna play some cards?"

"No, thanks," Galen said, slouching and swiveling in Maggie's chair.

"Well, wanna Netflix? I'm halfway through the third season of *Friday Night Lights*."

"How are we going to Netflix?"

Pete nodded at the laptop on Maggie's desk.

"Seriously?" Galen asked.

Pete nodded again.

"Does Maggie know? This is her personal computer, you know. Since the church computer was stolen."

Pete shrugged. "You're her husband. Surely you're allowed to touch her computer."

"All right then," Galen said, wiggling the mouse to bring the computer to life. "Let's see what Coach Taylor's been up to."

One and a half episodes later, the policeman appeared in the office doorway.

Galen and Pete looked up guiltily.

"Find it?" Pete asked.

The officer frowned. "No. Searched the room, didn't find anything but garbage. I just wasted an hour of my time."

Pete's face got red.

Galen jumped up. "We thank you for looking. I'm sure our guests will sleep easier tonight."

The officer grunted and headed for the door.

Pete swore at him as he went.

"Stop it, Pete. For crying out loud, do you know how much the police do for this church? Do you know how much we might need them in the future?"

Chapter 16

The school bus dropped the boys off at the church on Monday. The boys ran inside, and Daniel and Elijah ran to Daniel's room to play. Isaiah veered off to find his mother. He found her in the salon, blow-drying somebody's hair. She looked up. "Hi, sweetie! How was your day?" she half-hollered.

"Not good."

Tiny was on the couch, looking at a comic book. Isaiah flopped down beside him. "Where'd you get that, Tiny?"

"Maggie got the whole series for me, for my birthday."

"Oh, cool," Isaiah said.

"She got me this shirt too," Tiny said, stretching out the front of his T-shirt so that Isaiah could see.

Isaiah nodded, losing interest.

"Why, what happened, Isaiah?" Maggie asked over the roar of the dryer.

Isaiah looked at the woman in the chair. "I can wait till you're done."

"You can borrow it if you want," Tiny offered.

"The shirt? Might be a little big."

"No, the comic book. If you're old enough to read."

"I'm seven," Isaiah said indignantly. "Of course I can read." Isaiah unzipped his backpack, pulled out a worn paperback, and flipped it opened, as if to prove his literary chops.

As Isaiah read, Maggie finished straightening the woman's hair.

After she removed the cape with a practiced flourish, the woman stood and handed her a ten-dollar bill. "Wow! Thanks!" Maggie said, taking it. "I'll put this toward more color for next time."

"Awesome," the woman said, admiring her reflection. "I can't believe how much better I look!"

After the rejuvenated woman bounced out of the salon, Maggie crossed the room to sit beside her son. "What's up, sweetie?" she asked, kissing him on the head.

"We have to talk," he said stoically, putting his book down.

"Why? What's wrong?"

"The kids are picking on Daniel at school."

"What kids?" Tiny asked, leaning forward as if he was about to get up.

"No, Tiny," Maggie said. "They're just kids. We're not going to scare them to death." Then she looked back to Isaiah and repeated, "What kids?"

"Just some kids, not really our friends, although I did invite Alec to my birthday party, but anyway, they are making fun of Daniel, calling him 'the healer' and stuff. They punch him and say, 'Now heal that, healer' and then run off. One of them punched me and told him to heal me too."

Maggie's eyebrows went up.

"It's OK, Mom. It didn't hurt," Isaiah assured her.

Maggie sighed and put her arm around her son. "OK, sweetie. Thanks for telling me. I'll talk to your dad and see what he wants to do, but we'll definitely do something. You are right. This is not OK."

An hour later, Levi showed up at the office door. Maggie's eyes grew wide, and she looked at Tiny's chair as if to make sure he was still there. "How can I help you?" Maggie asked, without inviting Levi into the office.

He came in anyway. "I need a place to stay," Levi said, and sat down across from Maggie.

Maggie looked from Tiny to the door to her computer screen, anywhere but into Levi's eyes. As the awkward silence stretched beyond recovery, the door to Maggie's right opened, and Pastor Chris came out. "I just emailed you a new brochure," he said to Maggie, ignoring Levi completely. "Can you print out a few hundred copies, in color? The printer in my office is loud, and I need to make some phone calls." Without waiting for an answer, he turned to go back to his office.

"We're out of colored ink," she said.

He turned back around to look at her. "Why?"

"Why?" Maggie sassed. "Because we used it all. What do you mean, why?"

"OK fine. Can you please run to Walmart and get some more ink?"

"Do we have the money?" she asked. "Ink is expensive."

Chris seemed to be thinking hard about something. "You know what? Never mind. I'll just do it myself." He turned to go back into his office.

Maggie got up and caught the door as it was closing. "Hang on, I have to talk to you for a second." She paused to look at Tiny. "Make sure he doesn't go anywhere else in the church," she said, and Tiny nodded his understanding. Then she followed Chris into the office and closed the door the rest of the way.

"Look, if this is about the ink, I'm sorry," Chris started.

"No, it's not about the stupid ink. Look, I've got a situation here, and I'm not sure what to do. That man out there is trying to check in here. I have no idea whether he's truly in need, but I do know that he is not a nice man, and that he is Daniel's biological father, and that is the only reason why he's here."

Chris just stared at her. "And?"

"The problem is, we can't let him stay here, but I'm not sure how to say no to him, on what grounds. And I don't want to escalate the situation. I mean, Tiny can forcefully remove him from the property, but I'd rather avoid that if possible."

"So then, let him stay."

"We can't."

"Why not?" Chris sat down.

"Because he's going to upset Daniel and Daniel's mother."

"You mean the woman who has been living off this church for a decade? We certainly wouldn't want to upset *her*."

Maggie stood still, her eyes wide, her lips frozen. Finally, she found some words, but her voice wavered as she spoke them. "I don't know how to explain it, Chris. I just know that he's going to cause problems, and I know it's important to you to not have problems around here."

"Fine," Chris said, standing up so fast that his chair spun out from behind him. He stalked to the door, flung it open, took one step outside and said, "You can't stay here. Please get off the property." Then he went back into his office and slammed the door. Maggie narrowly made it outside of his office before the door was closed again, leaving Maggie and Tiny to stare at the stunned Levi.

"Why?" Levi managed after a few seconds.

Maggie sighed. "Just go, Levi."

"Not without talking to my son."

"Levi, go, or I will have Tiny carry you to the road."

Levi looked at Tiny and then at Maggie. "This isn't over," he said, and got up to leave.

"Wanna follow him outside?" Maggie asked, but Tiny was already on his way.

That night, at dinner, Maggie finally got a chance to catch Galen up on the day's news. She started with Levi.

"I've made it clear to Harmony that she and Daniel can stay here if she's scared of Levi," Galen said.

"Really?" Maggie asked.

Galen looked annoyed. "Yes, really. But just them two. The whole church isn't moving in."

"But does Harmony *really* know she's welcome? I think you've made it clear in the past that she's not."

Galen set his fork down. "Will you give me a break? I'm really trying here. Yes, I've made it clear. I don't know if she *feels* welcome, but she is. So … what else is going on?"

Maggie took a deep breath. "Kids are picking on Daniel at school," she said as she exhaled.

"Of course they are," Galen said.

"Well, we should do something about it."

Galen watched his sons eat for a minute. Then he said, "I'll go see Mrs. Little tomorrow, OK?"

"Thank you."

"But I'm not sure how much good it's going to do. People like Daniel have always been persecuted, throughout history. If he's going to go to school, he's going to get picked on. And I have a feeling that Daniel can handle it."

"Don't be so naive," Maggie said.

"Excuse me?"

"Daniel's just a kid. Being bullied leaves lasting scars. Just 'cause you were never bullied—"

"Oh, and you were?"

Maggie took a deep breath. "Look, I don't want to fight about it. I just want you to take this seriously. One of them punched Isaiah too—"

"I'm OK, Mom," Isaiah interjected.

Galen's face softened a little. "I do take it seriously. I really do. But how many emergencies can I handle at once? Dwight and Pastor got back today, so I'm waiting for the shoe to drop there. I've got to go to Bible study in a few minutes and I'm really not in the mood. We've got bills to pay, I'm behind in the garage, and I'm just … I'm just tired."

Isaiah stopped eating and looked at his dad. Then he pushed his chair away from the table and stood. He took two quick steps and then wrapped his small arms around his father's wide shoulders. "I love you, Dad."

Galen looked at Maggie, and then wrapped his arms around his son in kind. "I love you too, little man."

Isaiah, his face now pressed against his father's chest, mumbled, "Daniel will be OK. You don't have to worry about him."

Chapter 17

Galen did go talk to Mrs. Little the next day.

She offered him a seat, and Galen managed to squeeze his large frame into a small one-unit desk designed for a third grader.

"How can I help you today?" Mrs. Little asked sweetly.

"Well, it seems, and I know this isn't your fault, that Daniel, and by association, Isaiah, are being picked on. I know that boys will be boys, but I just wanted to see if we couldn't nip this in the bud before any real damage is done."

"I see," Mrs. Little said. "I wasn't aware that this was happening, but Daniel does behave much differently than the other children. I personally welcome the difference. He's very compliant and respectful, and he works hard at learning. But he's also very serious, always. And he quotes the Bible a lot."

Galen tried to squash a smile, but failed.

"But I will definitely keep a closer eye on him, especially at recess, and make sure that he is safe, and of course, that Isaiah is safe too. Your son is a really good friend to Daniel. He's a nice young man."

"Good. Thank you for saying so. I hope he is compliant and respectful as well?"

"Oh, absolutely." Mrs. Little smiled. "He's always respectful. And he's compliant except for during art class. I'm afraid he finds art to be a waste of his time."

Galen tried to squash another smile, more successfully this time. "OK, I wasn't aware. I'll talk to him about that. Thank you so much for your time, Mrs. Little."

"Oh, anytime. I wish all parents were as attentive and involved as you and your wife are."

Galen nodded and smiled, and then began the process of prying himself free of the desk.

When the boys got off the bus that day, Levi was waiting for them in the parking lot.

Daniel stopped in his tracks, and just looked at him.

Isaiah and Elijah ran past Levi, ignoring him completely, but then they noticed that their friend wasn't with them. Isaiah turned around. "Come on, Daniel!"

Daniel didn't answer. He didn't move either. He looked at the strange man in front of him.

"You're Daniel, right? Harmony's boy?" Levi asked.

Daniel nodded.

Levi took a step forward.

Daniel took a step back.

"You go on ahead," Isaiah said to Elijah. "We'll be right in." Elijah turned and ran toward the building.

"I'm your father, Daniel."

Daniel didn't even blink. "God is my only father."

Levi laughed. "I guess that's what you get when you grow up in a church. Look, kid, I am your father, and I could teach you a thing or two that you won't learn here. I don't know how you've been doing what you've been doing, but you're wasting it here. If you come with me, right now, you won't be homeless anymore. I can buy you whatever you want. You could be rich, kid, rich and famous."

"It is easier for a camel to pass through the eye of a needle than for a rich man to enter the kingdom of God," Daniel said.

Levi swore. He took two steps toward his son. Daniel stood his ground this time. "Look, that's enough of that crazy talk. I'm not talking about a camel. This is the real world, kid. How 'bout you come with me?" He took another two steps and tried to grab Daniel. Daniel darted out of the way.

A voice from behind spoke sharply and suddenly, "Daniel! Isaiah! You come here right this instant!"

Levi turned around to see Maggie coming down the church steps. Tiny was right behind her. Elijah stood on the steps, watching, looking scared. Daniel and Isaiah began to walk toward Maggie.

"You get out of here, right now, Levi, or I will call the police!" Maggie hollered.

Daniel turned around for a last look at the man who shared his DNA. "I will pray for you, sir, but don't come around here anymore. I will not throw my pearls before swine."

That night, at Bible study, Galen looked out at a congregation peppered with new faces. "I know a lot of you are new here, but I wanted to tell you a little bit about what's been going on here. I know a lot of you don't know young Daniel, but he is an eight-year-old who lives here, and he's something of a hero of mine.

"Daniel has a special relationship with Jesus. I mean, a lot of us do, but Daniel, well, he really knows how to put his confidence in God. Sometimes I envy him. And because of this confidence, God has worked through Daniel to do some pretty awesome things. Maybe you have heard about some of them. People have come to know Jesus because of Daniel. People have been physically healed because of Daniel.

"But recently, Daniel's biological father has come back into Daniel's life. It seems his sole motivation is to capitalize, to take advantage, to make money off Daniel. This is not the way God works, folks. I ask you for your help tonight and for the days to come. If any of you see anyone acting suspicious, please tell someone else right away. And let's all work together to keep an eye on all of the children here at church.

"Now, let's open our Bibles to Hebrews 13:5 ..."

At the end of the service, Galen gave an altar call, and two new people came forward. He prayed with each of them, and when he had finished, one of them asked to see Daniel. Galen beckoned Daniel forward. Daniel came. The man knelt again at the altar, and Daniel knelt beside him, one hand on the man's back, and the two prayed together for some unnamed pain.

The next morning, Maggie arrived at the office to find Tiny with fresh coffee and Pete sitting in her chair. "You're up early," she said to Pete. Then she took the coffee and thanked Tiny.

Pete hopped up and made a big show of offering her the seat. "I warmed it up for you. Yes, I am up early. Partly because it smells so bad in my room and partly because I couldn't wait to tell you the latest gossip."

Maggie looked at the pastor's door.

"Don't be ridiculous," Pete said. "He's not here yet. Tiny, shut the door."

Tiny shut the door, as Maggie took her coat off and sat. "Pete, it's wrong to gossip. I don't want to hear it."

"OK then, it's not gossip. It's just news. Dwight got hammered last night—"

"That's not news," Maggie said, turning on her computer.

"Let me finish!" Pete said. "He got hammered and he got to talking about *how much money* he and Pastor Chris raised in Connecticut."

"Oh yeah?" Maggie said, still not sounding very interested.

"Yeah, like thousands. I asked him how much exactly he'd seen, but then he realized he'd said too much and he shut up."

Maggie looked up into Pete's expectant gaze. "What's your point?"

"My point is, I thought Pastor was going to tell them how to start a shelter in their church? Did you know he was going to get money?"

"No, Pete. I don't know anything that goes on around here except who is sleeping here and what their allergies are. And sometimes I don't even know that. And I think I like being in the dark."

"Oh, stop it, Maggie! Don't you see? This could be our way out!"

"Our way out of what, Pete? Just what are you trying to accomplish?"

"Maggie! Winter is coming! This place is going to fill up just like it always does. You really want *Chris* running the show?" Pete added a few expletives to drive home his point.

"Don't say bad words," Tiny ordered.

"Yes, Tiny. Sorry," Pete said without looking at Tiny. "Maggie, if they raised money, where is it? The showers on the second floor haven't worked in months. We've eaten lima beans for six days in a row. No one's replaced your computer. Why aren't we seeing any improvements? Why aren't we seeing any *anything*? Isn't he getting paid for those television shows and those internet shows too?"

Maggie sighed. "Pete, you're probably right, but I really don't see what you or I can do about it. We have a treasurer. He's balancing the books. I've just got to trust God to balance the rest—"

She wasn't done talking, but Pete was done listening. "Fine. You're just too scared to do anything about it. Well, I'll tell you *what*. I am *not* scared of these people."

Later that morning, Maggie was in the salon coloring the hair of a woman she'd met at the bank. Tiny had just left to go to the bathroom, so Maggie looked incredibly nervous when Dwight appeared in the open doorway.

"You wanna tell me who's been going through my stuff?"

Maggie's hands started to shake, and she squeezed the coloring brush even tighter. She looked down at the woman's head. "I have no idea what you're talking about."

Dwight took a few steps into the salon. "I think you do. You know everything that goes on around here. Someone went through my room while I was gone. And I think you know who." He took two more steps closer. Maggie looked at her phone, which was now farther away from her than Dwight was. "And you're going to tell me who." Dwight took another step and was inches from Maggie. She stepped away from him and toward her phone just as Tiny reappeared in the doorway, still zipping up his pants.

"Get away from her!" he shouted and started toward Dwight.

Dwight stepped back from the open-mouthed bank teller and Maggie and put his hands up in the air. "OK, OK, I'm not doing anything. Just asking a question."

Tiny kept on coming until he was standing between Maggie and Dwight.

"How about you, big fella? Do you know who was in my room?"

"I don't know anything," Tiny said.

Dwight glared at Maggie for several long seconds and then turned and left.

"Everything OK?" the teller asked.

"Absolutely," Maggie said, letting go of a breath she'd been holding since Dwight had appeared. "Sorry about that."

"No worries. That guy was just scary."

"You're telling me," Maggie said. "Thanks, Tiny."

"You bet," Tiny said and returned to his couch and comic book.

Pastor Chris did eventually stroll into the office that afternoon, carrying a Starbucks cup, and Maggie did look at him suspiciously.

"Something wrong?" he asked her.

"You're going away this weekend too, right?"

"Yes. I'll be speaking at a church in Pittsburg," he said, flipping through his keys.

"And will you be taking Dwight?"

He stopped flipping and looked up at her. "Yes, why?"

Maggie feigned innocence. "I was just curious. You know, why you always take him. There's lots of guys around here who would love to go. And we've got some people who have moved on from here who could share their success stories, about how this church helped them."

Chris frowned. "Do *you* want to go with me?"

"Oh no!" Maggie hurried. "I was just wondering why you always take Dwight?"

"I take Dwight because he is a hero. He has a very moving testimony and he does a good job of sharing it." He unlocked his door and went inside.

Maggie stepped in the way of him closing the door. "But how does his testimony help you accomplish your goals?"

Chris leveled his gaze at her, seeming to really pay attention to her for the first time since they'd met. "What are you getting at, Ms. Turney? Did Dwight say something to you?"

Maggie looked emboldened. She took another step forward. "No, he didn't. It's more about what others are saying about Dwight."

"Oh yeah? Why don't you shut the door?"

"No, thank you," Maggie said. "People are saying that he was never actually in the service. Have you checked out any of his credentials?"

"You know what? That's a great idea! I'm going to do that right now. Thank you very much." He looked at his computer as if to dismiss her. She paused for several seconds as if she had something more to say. Then she turned and left his office, leaving the door open.

Chapter 18

On Sunday morning, the sanctuary was packed. More than a dozen new people had moved into the shelter over the previous week.

The JCTV cameras were off for the weekend, as Pastor Chris was away, and Elder George Clifford, his fill-in, wasn't quite television material. His sermon was well thought out and organized, and he read it from the page, mispronouncing many of the words, without ever looking up at his congregation. The men were yawning, the women were obviously daydreaming, and the children were either squirming or sleeping.

When the sermon finally ended, the worship team (this one borrowed from Lighthouse Church in Fairfield) took the stage, and Elder George struggled through an altar call. No one came forward, and he dismissed everyone with a dispassionate benediction.

When he had finished, most of the people filed out of the sanctuary and down to lunch. But one of the families headed toward Daniel and Harmony. Maggie looked at Galen for direction, and he nodded toward the door.

"Come on, boys, let's go see what's for lunch," Maggie said. Elijah hesitated, and Cari scooped him up and carried him toward the door.

A haggard-looking woman approached Daniel. She was carrying a toddler on one hip, and held the hand of another little girl.

"Is it true what they're saying about your son?" the woman asked Harmony.

Harmony looked surprised at the question and didn't answer her. The woman looked at Galen for an answer.

"Daniel is a young man after God's heart. If that's what you've heard about him, then it's true."

"You don't believe in God, do you?" Daniel asked the little girl.

She shrugged.

"What's your name?" he asked her.

"Alicia."

"OK, Alicia. Well, God is real. And his son Jesus is real. And Jesus died a long time ago so that you could live forever. Do you want to live forever?"

Alicia nodded.

"Come with me," Daniel said, and took the girl's hand. He led her to the altar and then they knelt side by side, Daniel's head only a few inches taller than hers.

"Is he healing her?" the mom asked.

"I think right now, he's leading her to Jesus. I think right now he's just helping her pray," Galen answered.

"I've never been religious," the woman explained. "Not even close. But we were in a shelter in Portland, and a woman there told us that Daniel had magical powers, that he could heal my little girl."

"What's wrong with her?" Harmony asked.

At the same time as Harmony spoke, Galen said, "There's nothing magical about Daniel. He'd be the first to tell you that God has been the one doing the healing. He's just using Daniel."

"So, it's true then?" the woman said to Galen.

Galen nodded. "I don't really understand it myself, but yes, it seems that many of Daniel's prayers have been answered."

The woman turned to Harmony. "She's been having headaches. Migraines, I think. I took her to a clinic, but the doctor told me to give her children's Tylenol. He didn't even seem to believe me. Acted like I was just after drugs or something. Anyway, it didn't work."

The toddler was squirming.

"You can put her down," Galen said. "She can't hurt anything around here. Let her burn off some of that energy."

"Are we going to miss lunch?" the woman asked.

Galen sat down. "I'll make sure that you don't. What is your name, other than 'Alicia's mom'?"

The woman smiled. She released the toddler, who immediately took off running. "I'm May." She sat down.

"It's good to meet you, May. When did you get here?" Galen asked.

"Just last night."

"Well then, welcome."

"Thanks," May said.

Harmony sat down too, beside May. Galen was seated in front of them, with his legs in the outside aisle, his upper body turned toward May. "So did you understand what George was saying this morning?"

"You mean the preacher?"

Harmony snorted. Galen ignored her. "Yeah. Did you understand what he was saying?"

May shook her head and looked down. "I wasn't really listening. Just waiting for it to be over."

Galen smiled. "OK. Will you listen to me for just a second? I'll make it super quick."

May glanced at her daughter, who was still kneeling beside Daniel. Then she looked into Galen's eyes and nodded.

"OK, so here's what I know to be true. God created people. We are not an accident. *You* are not an accident. But people, well, we often tend to choose ourselves over our Creator. We often make selfish decisions. We choose to make ourselves happy instead of making God happy. Well, God is pure good. He always has been. So he can have nothing to do with bad. He can't look at bad. He can't be close to bad. And our selfishness is very bad. So, God has a son. His name is Jesus. Jesus came to earth many years ago, and he lived as a man for about thirty years. He left heaven and became a person, so he went through many, if not all, of the same things you're going through in your life. But the difference is, Jesus never once made a selfish decision. From the time he was born, he never once chose his own happiness over God's. Does that make sense?"

May nodded.

"OK, so because of our badness, we don't deserve to be close to God. But Jesus was close to God. He was perfect. So he gave his life. He died a horrible death, voluntarily, so that we could be close to God. He paid the price that we should have been charged, so that we could be forgiven. Once you pray to Jesus, and tell him that you believe, tell him that you thank him for his sacrifice, tell him that you're sorry for your selfishness, then through Jesus, you can be close to God again."

"OK," May said immediately.

"OK?" Galen asked. "Would you like to pray that prayer?"

May nodded. "Do I have to go up there?" She nodded toward the altar.

"Only if you want to."

She shook her head.

"OK then, we can pray right here, if you want to."

May nodded again.

"All right. I'm going to say a prayer, and if you want to, you can repeat it after me. You can say it out loud or silently, but know that it only matters if you really mean it. This isn't a magic trick either."

May smiled. "I understand."

"OK then." Galen closed his eyes and leaned forward on his knees, bowing his head. Harmony closed her eyes and bowed her head too. May looked at her daughter at the altar, and then she followed suit.

"Father in heaven," Galen began. May immediately repeated his words. "Thank you for creating me." May softly echoed. "I understand that I have done selfish things, things that have hurt you, things that the Bible calls sin." He paused to let May speak. She did. Galen continued, "Jesus, thank you for coming to earth and for dying on the cross for me. I ask you now to come into my life. I ask you to forgive me of my sins. I want to know you. Through you, I want to know God." May repeated every word. "Amen," Galen said.

"Amen," May repeated.

When they all opened their eyes, Daniel and Alicia stood in front of them, still holding hands. "Alicia is going to heaven now," Daniel said. "I also think that her headaches will stop."

May began to cry. She reached out and scooped her daughter out of Daniel's hand and into her own arms. "I love you so much, honey," she said to her daughter. Then she looked at Galen over her daughter's shoulder and said, "I feel weird. Different. Lighter, I think."

Galen smiled. "Yep, that often happens. Do you have any other questions, about God, Jesus, the Bible?"

"I'm hungry," Alicia said.

May laughed. "I don't think so. Not right now."

"OK, no problem. Let me or Maggie know if you do have any questions. In the meantime"—he reached for a pew Bible—"keep this, and start reading the Book of John. Feel free to write in it or highlight anything you want to remember or want to talk about later."

May took the Bible in one hand. "OK, thank you."

"You are very welcome."

May let her daughter go and stood up. "Uh-oh, I lost the other one," she said.

Harmony laughed. "She's right over there," she said, pointing to a window.

"Thanks," May said, and went to retrieve her youngest. "Sometimes she tries to escape," she said, grabbing her off the windowsill.

"Don't we all," Harmony muttered.

Galen, Harmony, and Daniel watched them leave the sanctuary. "Well, that was pretty great," Harmony said.

"Yep," Daniel quickly agreed. "And that might not have happened if Chris had been here. Guess I'm glad he's off being a big deal." Daniel shoved his hands in his pockets and headed toward the door.

On Tuesday afternoon, Pete was outside sitting in the smoking section.

Annie joined him. "That looks comfy," she said, nodding at his rusty metal folding chair.

"Yeah, well, beggars can't be choosers," he said, and took another drag off his cigarette.

"You know, we aren't supposed to be out here." She perched on the edge of a boulder.

"Yeah well, when the *pastor* is away, the mice will play. There's more metal chairs in the kitchen."

"That's OK. I've got some natural padding here. Got a smoke?"

Pete was obviously annoyed. "Why don't you have any?" He held his pack of 1839s out to her.

"I did," she said, taking one. "Some jerk kiped them." Annie swore a few times to accentuate her disgust. "You know what we need around here?"

"Cheap housing?" Pete offered.

Annie laughed as she lit her cigarette. She took a deep, grateful drag and then exhaled. "Yeah, that too. We also need a new pastor."

Pete snorted. "Well, yeah. But I think that ship has sailed."

"What does that mean?"

"I mean, I think we missed our chance. The *elders* hired Chris before we could get someone good."

"Well, then why don't we fire him?"

Pete looked at her as if she was nuts. Just then Kevin joined their huddle. Without looking up at him, Pete said, "I'm all out. Don't even ask." Then he said to Annie, "We are a bunch of bums. I don't see how we're going to fire anyone. Just because we live here doesn't mean we have any say. Haven't you noticed that? We don't have a say about anything."

Kevin turned and went into the building.

"Stupid mooch," Pete muttered as he went. "That guy has never bought a smoke of his own."

"Maybe we can't do anything about it. But G and Maggie can. Or Cari. Or even Gertrude. Why aren't they doing anything?"

Pete laughed. "What do you expect them to do? Stage a coup?"

Annie shrugged and tapped her ashes off. "I don't know. I just know this sucks, and G would make such a good pastor."

Kevin returned then with his own metal chair.

"Still don't have any cigarettes," Pete said without looking up.

"That's OK. Annie, you got any?"

Annie shook her head.

"You guys talking about G taking over?"

"Sort of," Pete said. "I don't think he can, and I don't even think he wants to. The guy's a mechanic."

"So?" Annie said defensively. "He's still a better preacher than Chris the fish."

Duke and Joyce joined the small group then. "What're you doin' out here in the cold?" Pete asked Joyce. "You don't even smoke."

Joyce's cheeks blushed as she gazed at Duke.

"What're you guys scheming?" Duke asked, and sat down on the boulder beside Annie.

Joyce glared at her. Duke gave Kevin a cigarette and then lit one of his own.

"Nothing," Pete said. "Just wishing we could get G to take over the preachin' and put Chris on the next outbound bus."

Duke laughed. "That would be great, actually. You should talk to him, Pete."

"To who? G? What am I supposed to say? Hey, you should stop working on cars and actually getting paid to come take care of us bums? Yeah, that's quite a job offer."

"What if we all talked to him together?" Annie said.

"What, like an intervention?" Pete joked. He took another cigarette out of his almost full pack and used his spent butt to light it. Kevin glared at him.

"I don't know," Annie said. "But if we all talked to him, maybe he'd do it."

"As in, maybe we could guilt him into it? Sorry, I like G too much for that," Pete said.

"Well," Kevin said, "Chris gets paid, right? Why couldn't G get paid?"

Pete spat into the dirt. "Chris gets paid 'cause he's on TV and because he drives all over the countryside preaching about how to love on homeless people."

"He gets paid for that?" Kevin asked.

"How do you think he affords that shiny new truck?"

"I dunno," Kevin admitted.

"Please?" Annie said, looking at Pete pleadingly. "Can we just talk to him? We could do it tonight, at Bible study."

"Fine," Pete said, standing up and stretching his back. "We can talk to him, but I don't think it's going to change anything. I don't think he can just take the job, even if he wants to, and I highly doubt he will want to. He'd have to be nuts."

Galen arrived for Bible study five minutes after it was supposed to start. He walked into the unusually quiet sanctuary and headed straight for the front. "Evening, everybody," he said jovially.

No one answered. This was strange. He turned and looked at them expectantly. "What's up?"

Pete stood up and cleared his throat. He took the three steps necessary to put him right beside Galen. "We've been talking, G, and we were wondering ..." Pete fidgeted, looking around as if waiting for someone to save him. "Well ..."

"What is it, Pete?" Galen looked unnerved.

"Well, we were wondering if you would consider being our pastor?"

Galen laughed. "What? What are you talking about?"

Pete cleared his throat again. "I think we all know that Chris isn't really working out."

There was some displeased murmuring among the guests.

"And, well," Pete continued, "I think we all know you'd be better at it. You'd do a better job."

Galen sighed and looked around. "I appreciate the vote of confidence, guys, but I can't just become the pastor. There's no job opening. Instead of trying to replace Chris, we need to be praying for—"

"Oh bull," Pete interrupted. "If you don't want the job, G, just say so, but don't feed us some line about supporting Chris. That guy is useless, and you know it."

Galen sighed. "Thank you for sharing, Pete. Now, if you will all open your Bibles to Hebrews 13:17."

Chapter 19

Chris and Dwight returned to Open Door on Thanksgiving morning. And even though Jessica (along with Pete, Maggie, and Cari) worked all morning to have a Thanksgiving feast on the table by one o'clock, when one o'clock came, Chris and Dwight were nowhere in sight.

"Do you want to say grace?" Maggie asked her husband as she wiped her hands on a frayed apron.

"Uh, sure," Galen said, looking around to find someone more qualified.

"We should let Daniel say grace," Isaiah piped up.

"No," Daniel said quickly. "G can do it."

"All right then," G began. "Let's bow our heads. Father in heaven, we thank you for this day that encourages us to really focus on our gratitude. Thank you for all the food that has been provided for us here and thank you for the people who prepared it for us. We thank you for your provision and protection. Amen."

There was a short-lived stampede toward the food line.

"Easy!" Maggie tried. "There's plenty for everyone!"

"Got to get there first, or there's no cranberry sauce!" Tiny explained too loudly.

Daniel was staring at Galen.

"You going to get in line, buddy?" Galen asked.

Daniel shook his head. "Is that what you pray in the morning, when you're walking around?"

"Yeah," Galen said, ruffling Daniel's hair. "Something like that."

"Can I pray with you tomorrow?"

Galen looked surprised. "You want to go outside with me?"

"Yeah, I want to walk around and pray, like you do."

"OK, sure. You've got to get up early, though."

"I'll be up," Daniel promised and then he ran to the end of the line.

Galen's family stayed for Bible study that night, so as Galen took his spot up front, the front row was full of his family, and his extended family, Harmony and Daniel.

Galen read from Philippians 4, and talked about how the key to true gratitude is contentment. "I know it can be difficult to be grateful when you are struggling just to get by," Galen said, "but that might be the very best time to give thanks. When you are in need, you are most dependent on God. That's when he really has an opportunity to bless you."

The guests, even the new ones, listened attentively to Galen, and when he gave the altar call, several people came forward, including a few people who had only recently come to stay at the shelter.

One of the new people was an attractive young woman, and as she knelt at the altar, she began to weep. Galen was already praying with someone else, and Daniel got up from his seat and knelt beside her. He reached up and put his small hand on her back and then bowed his head, speaking softly to her.

Everyone else finished praying, but Daniel and the young woman stayed. Everyone waited patiently for them to finish, everyone that is, but Dwight. Dwight was fidgeting in his seat and making his impatience known with a series of exaggerated sighs. Finally, Galen looked at him, but Dwight didn't return his stare. He just kept wiggling in his seat, looking increasingly agitated.

"Look, if you've got to go to the little girls' room, just go," Duke said, and several people laughed.

Dwight swore at Duke and just kept fidgeting.

Finally, the young woman and Daniel stood up. The woman, keeping her head down, headed straight for the door. "Maggie," Daniel said from the front of the room, "could you please go with her and call the police?"

"Of course," Maggie said, surprised, and she jumped up to follow her out of the room.

Dwight stood up. "Nobody's calling the cops."

The woman stopped walking so quickly that Maggie almost ran into her.

"Everybody, just sit down," Dwight said.

"What's going on, buddy?" Galen asked Daniel.

"That man," Daniel said boldly, pointing at Dwight, "hurt her. We need to call the police."

Galen nodded at Maggie. "Get her out of here."

Maggie started moving again, taking the shaken woman by her shoulders.

"I said, don't move," Dwight snapped, and from the back of his waist he pulled out a handgun and leveled it at Maggie.

There was a collective gasp, and the people in the back rows began to run out of the room. "Everyone sit down!" Dwight hollered, but the fleeing people ignored him. He swung the gun in their direction, but only briefly. Within seconds, it was pointed again at Maggie, and the two dozen people who had been seated behind him had fled to safety.

The two dozen people in front of him, however, were crouching on the floor. Isaiah lay on top of his brother, and began to pray. Mothers pressed crying children into the carpet and pleaded with them to stop whimpering. Only Chief remained in his seat, and he turned toward Dwight without fear. "That'll be enough, you fool. You're not gonna shoot anyone." Chief called Dwight a few names that insulted his masculinity, and Dwight swung the gun toward Chief. Chief stood up to face Dwight, apparently fearless.

"Shut up, old man," Dwight said through clenched teeth.

Maggie urged her charge forward a few feet, but Dwight saw their movement out of the corner of his eye and swung the gun back toward them. "I said, stop! No one is calling the police."

"What are you going to do?" Chief asked. "Murder us so no one reports you? Does that really make sense? Just how many bullets you got in that gun?"

"Stop, Chief," Daniel said gently. "He doesn't understand."

Dwight held the gun on the women, but turned his eyes to glare at Daniel. "Shut up, you stupid little freak."

"Shh," Galen tried to hush Daniel.

"It's OK," Daniel said to Galen. The young boy took two steps toward the man with the gun. "I know you don't understand, Dwight. I know you've been lying every day. I know that hurts. But the only thing that can fix this is Jesus. You have to talk to him. You have to—"

Dwight charged toward the boy, completely forgetting about the women, who fled for the door as Dwight pointed the revolver at the child. "Shut up, for once, will you just shut up, I'm going to kill you," Dwight said, showing no signs of slowing his advance on Daniel.

Galen threw his body between Daniel and Dwight, and Dwight, his face red, his eyes ice cold, pulled the trigger.

A lot happened in the seconds that followed.

Galen immediately crumpled to the floor. His hands flew to his chest, and he made a moaning sound that sounded surprised and weak. Young Daniel fell to his knees beside Galen and put both his small hands over Galen's large ones just as Galen's eyes closed.

As Galen fell, Chief tackled Dwight from the side. Both men went down, and the gun flew out of Dwight's hand. Chief leapt off the man and scrambled for the gun. By the time Dwight had righted himself, Chief had already checked to make sure he had another bullet. Then he pointed the gun at Dwight. "If you move, at all, I will shoot you in the head. Please, give me the chance. Jail's not much worse than this place. I wouldn't mind a change of scenery."

As the nearest patrol car headed toward the church, as the EMTs dropped their sandwiches and jumped in their ambulance, as Maggie ran back into the sanctuary, screamed in grief, and fell at her husband's side, Galen was already somewhere else.

The light was blinding, and Galen's instinct was to squint, but then he realized he didn't need to. The light felt warm, inviting, magnificent. He searched the light for something he might recognize, something he might understand, and then he saw a face appearing, a face so familiar he instantly recognized it, even though he'd never seen it before. "Savior," Galen breathed, and the face smiled.

"Son."

Galen felt tears sliding down his cheeks. "I thought there were no tears in heaven."

"You're not in heaven," Jesus answered. "You're not done on earth yet."

Galen felt a pain in his heart then, as if it was being pulled in two different directions. "I don't want to go."

"I know. But I'm asking you to. My sheep need you. Go, feed my sheep. I'll see you again soon."

Galen's chest felt as if it was going to explode. He gasped for air as he'd never gasped before, as if he'd been underwater for far too long, and the air came rushing into his chest so fast it burned, and then he gasped again, his mouth open, he gulped and gulped for more air, more sweet, delicious, scorching air.

The first thing he heard after Jesus' voice was his wife's. "Galen, can you hear me?" As he listened to her voice, it grew closer, and he opened his eyes to find her teary emerald eyes only inches from his own. Instinctively, he reached one hand up to her, and she laughed through the tears. Galen laid his hand on her hair and stroked it as he shifted his gaze to his sons, who were now sitting on the floor staring at him. They had obviously been crying too. Then Galen looked at Daniel, who still had his two small hands pressed to Galen's chest. His eyes were squeezed shut, and his lips were moving silently.

Galen looked down at his chest, but there was nothing there. No wound. No blood. Only a small hole in his shirt. He sat up, still looking around, but there was no evidence to support the pain he had felt.

He looked at the guests, all rising from their spots on the floor, slowly, as two police officers rushed in, with two paramedics right behind them. The paramedics rushed to Galen, who tried to hold them off. "I'm OK, I'm OK," he said.

"What happened to you?" one of them asked.

It did look kind of strange. He was still sitting on the floor, with a young boy and a woman crouched over him as if he was dying.

"I was ... I was ..." he looked around as if looking for words to say. "I was ... nothing. I'm OK, I think." With both hands he felt his own chest, and, sure enough, it was a chest, his own chest, as solid and whole as it had ever been.

"Did you fall?" the paramedic asked.

"Yes," Galen said with a chuckle. "I fell all right."

The paramedic checked him over, but finding nothing wrong with him, asked, "Do you need to go to the hospital?"

"No, no, I don't think so," Galen said.

The paramedic looked around the room. "Was anyone else hurt?"

No one answered at first. Then Daniel said softly, "There's a woman here. She's been hurt."

"Oh yeah, she's in the office," Maggie said, not looking away from her husband.

The police arrested Dwight, and this time, Chris did not come to his aid. This time, Dwight was charged with multiple crimes. This time, the police learned that not only had Dwight never served overseas, he had been dishonorably discharged after less than a year of service.

Within days of his arrest, Dwight began to share what used to be secrets. Apparently, there had been a lot of money in a church safe, a safe that had disappeared one night only hours after Dwight had told his second cousin about said safe.

And Dwight had a lot to say about Pastor Chris, the elders, and their accounting practices, and while no charges were filed, Chris was quick to resign. The church in Haileyville, Connecticut asked that their financial support be returned, and JCTV quickly canceled Chris's contract.

Galen asked the elders to formally resign as members, and they, who had heard stories about what had really happened that Thanksgiving evening, spoke to Galen as if they were spooked he was speaking back.

They couldn't get out of that church fast enough.

Pete, Maggie, and Cari spent a single afternoon together writing new bylaws and then formally offered Galen the job of pastor.

He accepted.

Annie formed a new worship team made up of church guests. She had more than enough volunteers. Tiny even wanted to join, so she told him he could play the triangle.

Pete took over half the Bible studies.

Galen hung a sign at his garage that said, "Open Fridays and Saturdays only. Call 555-3399 for emergency towing." The Turney family moved into the parsonage, which, though small, was far more spacious than their apartment had been.

And Daniel stopped healing people. He didn't do so consciously, and he never stopped believing that if God wanted to heal someone through him, he still could. But for a while anyway, God was choosing not to present those scenarios.

Epilogue

Each morning, before Galen has his coffee, he meets Daniel outside the parsonage door, and together, they walk around the property, praying together, all four of their hands in the air.

As the months go by, Daniel's hands get a little higher, a little closer to the height of Galen's.

One fall morning, nearly four years after the shooting, Daniel meets Galen at his door and asks, "How much longer do you think you can keep this up?"

Galen laughs. "Oh, it is exhausting, that's for sure. Still wondering why God picked me. And I can see why Pastor Dan's heart gave out."

Daniel smiles and looks up at his friend. "Well, the way I figure it, you have to last another ten years."

"Oh yeah? Why's that?"

"Because I'm going to Bible college. And then I'm going to come back here and help you. Then you can retire if you want."

Galen smiles. "Oh I can, can I?"

"Yep. That's my plan."

"It's a good plan," Galen says.

"Thanks."

"You ready?"

"Yep, let's go."

And then the pastor and his young friend begin to walk the familiar path around the church property—with their hands in the air, they thank God for his protection, for his provision, for his love, and for his miracles.

***

More Books by Robin Merrill

SHELTER TRILOGY
Shelter
Revival

PIERCEHAVEN TRILOGY
Piercehaven
Windmills
Trespass

STANDALONE CHRISTIAN STORIES
Commack
Grace Space: A Direct Sales Tale

WING AND A PRAYER MYSTERIES
The Whistle Blower
The Showstopper
The Pinch Runner

GERTRUDE, GUMSHOE COZY
MYSTERY SERIES
Introducing Gertrude, Gumshoe
Gertrude, Gumshoe: Murder at Goodwill]
Gertrude, Gumshoe and the VardSale Villain
Gertrude, Gumshoe: Slam Is Murder
Gertrude, Gumshoe: Gunslinger City
Gertrude, Gumshoe and the Clearwater Curse

DEVOTIONALS
The Jesus Diet: How the Holy Spirit Coached Me to a 50-Pound Weight Loss
More Jesus Diet: More of God, Less of Me, Literally

Robin also writes sweet romance as Penelope Spark.

Discussion Questions

- Galen refused to fill out a formal membership application. Why do you think that is? Do you agree with his decision? Why or why not? How do you think churches should manage membership?

- Could you relate to Galen's reluctance to step into Pastor Dan's shoes? What do you think held him back?

- Did Daniel remind you of a child you know or have known? Share about this child.

- What can we learn about "childlike faith" from Daniel?

- Galen didn't want Harmony and Daniel staying in his home. Did you agree with his decision? Why or why not?

- How do you think a group of believers should handle a "bully" like Chief?

- What can a group of believers do to protect themselves from "wolves in sheep's clothing"?

- Upon first hearing that Dwight might have a gun, Galen investigated the situation for himself before calling the police. Did you agree with his decision? Why or why not?

- Have you ever experienced or witnessed a physical healing similar to those Daniel was a part of? Share your story.

- How do you think Maggie has grown since *Shelter*?

- What do you think Daniel's future holds?